Out of my BOX

A collection of powerful literary pieces by women writers

WriteFluence

Contents

Foreword

WriteFluence features worthy authors and show-cases their talent. We believe in building authors into brands and giving aspiring writers the opportunity to expand their wings.

While our writing community is built up on our Instagram page, we also offer literary services viz. publishing consultation, book interior and cover designing, proofreading, author branding and book promotions.

'Out of my BOX' is a compilation of winning short stories that were selected from the 79 submissions received for **FemmeFluenza,** our first exclusively-for-women creative writing contest held on the occasions of International Women's day, 2021.

The book comprises of 23 stunning literary pieces by women writers, each of which are one better than the other. We hope you enjoy reading all the stories as much as we enjoyed compiling them.

Happy reading!

Acknowledgements

Thank you to all the writers and participants who made FemmeFluenza 2021 a successful event.

Rubatosis

By Prakhar Patidar

They sat on the ledge with their legs hanging in the open. It was a small town. One could tell by the sea of small houses all around; roof after roof, gapped by narrow streets running in between, intersecting oddly like a shoddy map. There wasn't a single tall building in sight. Just one or two-storied houses and an occasional four-storied structure. A sea of low-level yellow and white lights. This house stood next to where Bitti lived: built on the ground floor with an open roof and a single room on top. And though not that high, sitting on that ledge made her heart race a bit. And despite the erratic beating of her heart, she sat there frequently with Simmi. Simmi, the more adventurous of the two, always had stories of hearts racing for far better reasons than sitting on a ledge barely 15ft above the ground.

Today, Simmi had done something ballsy. Very brave for the small town. Bitti knew she had gone out with that boy from class, but for details, she'd have to pester Simmi. She had known Simmi for enough years to know her antiques. They had been neighbors for all 16 years of their lives.

She tugged on her kurta to initiate the pestering. Simmi slyly sat there enjoying every bit of it. She acted as if there was nothing to tell. It was simple: she had just gone to the cinema hall. There was nothing special about it; it was just one of the few spaces where holding hands, and more with a date was possible. Bitti began to get annoyed.

"We were a bit late. We missed the beginning. Then Varun missed more of it because he went to get some popcorn."

"You always make him get popcorn."

Simmi shrugged and continued, "He offers. Anyway, we picked the wrong film because even for a weekday- morning show, the theatre was pretty crowded."

"As if you would have done anything."

Bitti saw Simmi's lips curve into a familiar smile. The lopsided-twinkly-eyed smile she was known for.

"You don't know that. You don't know the things we have done."

Whenever Simmi got candid about things not meant to be spoken about candidly, Bitti got a mini heart attack. The same old fear that always lived deep in her stomach......of being caught. But being caught doing what? Talking? Speaking their hearts? She didn't know. She just knew whenever this feeling in her stomach began to bloat: something wrong was happening. It always took her back to the time when she had first experienced this bloating fear. A few years ago, at one of the family gatherings, the whole family sat in their living room talking. The television was on, another noise added to the already loud conversation taking place. The adults were talking, the younger kids were busy running around the house, and the teens had their eyes glued to the television. A romantic-comedy was on. It was the time when Hindi cinema had just begun getting bolder with depictions of romance. The actors danced cozily alone in the frame: almost to the beating of her own heart, it seemed. In each other's arms: inhaling each other's breath. With each moment of increased proximity between them, something happened deep in Bitti's stomach. She couldn't explain it. It just felt good. It made her want to be in the frame in place of either of the actors; it didn't matter. She just wanted to see where this calling that came from her stomach took her. As the actors locked lips, Bitti suddenly realized where she was. Her mother was looking at her: locked lips on-screen and locked eyes at home. That is when her stomach began to feel bloated. The look on her mother's face was that of disgust amalgamated with embarrassment. She didn't have to do anything more than widen her eyes and jerk her head in a quick, short motion, and Bitti jumped onto her feet to switch the television off. She felt naked. Her mother had caught her in something she couldn't describe aptly yet, but now she had a feeling she was supposed to be ashamed of it. Later her mother took her to a corner to give her an earful to confirm this suspicion. It was mostly about how such indecent crap is not for a house full of people, but she knew the underlying anger was about how whatever Bitti felt then had crept on her face in red.

Bitti immediately hushed Simmi. They sat too close to the room on the roof: Simmi's brother's room. She didn't want him to know what should stay between them. It was a strange feeling, but she was getting used to it, an afraid stomach and a heart beating to curiosity, if hearts sit deep in one's stomach.

"Shhhh. Someone will hear you! Your brother's room is practically 5 feet away."

"Yeah, but he isn't here."

"Where is he? It's late."

"I don't know. Somewhere. Boys can be anywhere. So I was saying we__"

"But still! He__"

"He's not important! Do you want to know what happened or not?"

Bitti wanted to know. Simmi's outings were a shared adventure for both of them: for Simmi the real experience of it, and Bitti was just happy in listening to the retellings of them. Simmi was seeing this boy from school, Varun. He seemed to like her a lot. Bitti was not sure if Simmi reciprocated the liking to a similar extent. She decided not to form an opinion just yet. It was fairly new, this romantic venture of Simmi and Simmi was never the one to give straight answers. Bitti had to wait and find clues in what Simmi chose to tell about him, how she spoke about him, all those micro-expressions when she did to piece an answer together. She joked she had gotten in good practice of reading people just because of Simmi's mischievously secretive nature.

"Yes, sorry. So Varun went to get popcorn…"

"Yeah, he got the popcorn, and this is like 30 minutes into the film, so he is the only person standing in the hall. Some loser yells at him. For literally walking to his seat!"

"Who?"

"I don't know. For sure some frustrated uncle. So now I yell back to shut him up. It's dark so no one could figure out who yelled."

"That's classic of you. Like a charging bull at the mildest of reds."

"They ask for it. Unlike you, with this unlady-like act of mine, Varun was very impressed."

"Did he say so?"

"He showed it. There were people all around, and yet he sat with his hand around my shoulder. The. Whole. Show."

It was surprising to Bitti. Varun was a visibly shy guy. It had taken him so long to approach Simmi.

And when he did, it was not without help. It was not like Simmi didn't know. Varun was not very stealthy with those longing looks. She just had the patience for him to take his time. When he finally mustered the courage to walk up to her after school and ask her to have kulfi with him, all Simmi said was: about time, and started walking in the direction of the kulfi-wala even before he could respond.

"That's so unlike him though", said Bitti.

"I swear. Had it been a big city or he been braver, he would have kissed me."

"How is yelling at an old grump romantic?"

"Don't count the causes but look at the effect".

"Yes, I will, when it'll happen for real", Bitti teased.

"It did! I swear on our friendship. And you wouldn't believe how fast my heartbeat went."

"He did that? Really?; her tone serious and heart fluttering. Simmi just nodded."

"The whole time?"

Simmi nodded earnestly.

"That out-of-control heartbeat you're talking about is fear. How much do you want to bet one of your Papa's acquaintances was sitting there too."

"I don't want to lose money. But I am telling you it wasn't fear. It was something different. Kind of like fear but in a good way."

"Did anything else happen?"

"Do you think this was not enough? But Bitti, you have to experience it once. Why don't you acknowledge Bablu's obvious moves? They are so obvious. He likes you so much."

"It has to be a two-way street, Simmi. With Bablu, it's a one-way highway. And I know what that kind of beating of the heart is. I think I do."

Bitti shifted nervously to find a more comfortable position. She had never spoken about it out loud. Simmi looked at Bitti hopefully, waiting for her to continue. She knew Bitti well too. She knew there would be no point in pushing her. She'd only retreat. She needed her time. In the nervousness and anticipation, both didn't hear the approaching footsteps.

"What do you think you do?"

It was Simmi's older brother. He didn't intend to sneak upon them. He merely walked up to them, but the effect was such that he startled both the girls. They felt they could have fallen off the ledge in SHOCK. Bitti didn't wait for the showdown that was to happen between the siblings. She regretted she ever said anything, got off the ledge, and walked off, this time her heart syncing with her feet. Simmi wasn't just going to walk away. Her brother smelled of cigarettes, but she didn't mention it. He knew they were talking about the boy he saw Simmi walk into the cinema hall with, but he didn't bring it up.

"Why do you always do that?" she spat, although not very vehemently. Just the usual resentment siblings share. Her brother just shrugged. "She was about to tell me something important. Couldn't you be a minute late, better yet the whole night?

You scared her away."
"She's not a cat. She chose to leave. She always leaves. I think she doesn't like me."
"No one likes you."
"Thank you for leaving the door unlocked.
Bitti had begun to climb down the stairs, but she could still catch the smile in his voice. A similar one sat on her lips.

In situations like these; that involved her heart and her stomach, sat fear camping under shame. Simmi had been the one to let her know it didn't have to be that way: that her heart could beat loud enough to feel like it sat in her ears, that it was okay to be led where the depth of her stomach wanted her to go. And yet Bitti could never. The time never felt right. She was too close to home, too seen in her hometown, too afraid to disappoint her mother. It was too much risk. And it was never meant to be what girls could do in the first place. Not good girls, at least. She didn't need another reminder of it. And so things went by, living and learning through Simmi's experiences and barely ever after that. Things also didn't slow down for her either. Simmi's family relocated to a different state soon afterward.

When Bitti got engaged four years later, she automatically dialed Simmi's number. Simmi came a week before the wedding, sat with Bitti on the same ledge where they had left a conversation unfinished; of attraction and related things. Made available to Bitti via some ticket now that she was getting married.

On her wedding night, she sat all pretty and poised, exactly like they show it in the films. Waiting for the same old calling to act up like it did on a whiff of cigarette smoke once. Instead, it was just the unsettling awareness of her own heartbeat and nothing else.

*rubatosis - n. the unsettling awareness of your own heartbeat

A Woman who knows too much

By Aditi Jain

"**B**eware of her."
The old granny tells them, eyes wide, her wrinkled face twisted in disgust.

"Is she evil?"

"God would know. She has not brought any harm to our people yet. But yes, the girls who do not obey their fathers, the girls who seek too much, she takes them away. Elders believe she sacrifices them on the altar for her rituals."

They say she lives in the shrine built at the outskirts of the village, near the dark, wild forest. Nobody dares to venture out there, lest she may curse them. Not even the strongest warriors who have won great battles and survived worst calamities.

Anoma was a child of a bright and curious mind. She had questions, opinions and everything a girl wasn't allowed to have.

"Girls should not ask questions. They should be quieter. Seen, but not heard."

Her grandmother would say, hushing her everytime she would wonder out loud 'why is the sky blue?'

It was a warm day, the sun was shining and the kids of the village were running around the fields, happy and gaily. Anoma was among them, following her mates, laughing and loving the way her dark hair would spill when the wind whipped against her face.

It is then her eyes fall on it, a beautiful butterfly with the bluest of the richest blues on its wings, gently flapping in a fields of yellows and greens and pinks. Anoma, mesmerized by the creature, follows it, unknowingly crossing the uncharted territory of the abomination.

The butterfly comes to rest on a flower, Anoma crouches and stares at it, marvelling.

"It's beautiful? Isn't it?"

The voice feels like a whisper, calm and soft.

"It is!" Anoma exclaims in childish excitement and whirls around. And instantly, all colour drains off from her face.

Behind her stands a tall figure, a staff in hand. Dark heavy cloak over majestic red robes - the woman's presence was unmistakable.

Anoma jumps up, almost stumbling and takes a

few panicked steps away from the lady. Her lip quivers, hardly able to breathe, she squeaks out.

"Sorry! I didn't mean to come here! I'm really sorry! Please forgive me!" She sobs, "I didn't come here on purpose! It's just that-" she vaguely gestures to the butterfly which was already humming away at some other flower"- it was-"

"Beautiful? Is it not?" The woman says again, cutting her off.

Anoma nods and stays silent, shivering in fear. Her father had told her to not go playing out today and she had disobeyed him.

Will I be punished now? Will she take me to the altar and sacrifice me to please the god?

She stays still, unmoving due to her terror. Even though her eyes are not visible, Anoma could feel her peering stare. Moments pass before the woman speaks again.

"Menelaus Blue."

The lady says, tilting her head towards the winged creature. "You can stay here more if you wish. But I should be going now."

She turns back and Anoma watches as her long and dark luscious hair sway to the rhythm of the wind. She walks away, disappearing behind the doors of her shrine, and the girl lets out a shaky exhale of relief. It is only when she is chopping vegetables for the supper, she makes a startling discovery.

Menelaus Blue was the name of the butterfly she saw that day. And when Father points the smile she has on her face, Anoma doesn't whisper a word of the lady.

"Is she evil?"

Anoma asks, as her grandmother tucks her into the bed.

"Who?"

"Her."

It takes a moment for her old woman to process her question. Anoma observes her face go pale and then twist into this hideous monstrosity that for a second it makes Anoma wonder if this woman is really her grandmother.

She barks fiercely, in a way that promises pain.

"You! You did not-"

"No I didn't! I'd never do that."

Anoma lies through her teeth, pulling the covers up to her chin.

The old woman sighs before her features morph into something familiar again.

"Listen, child, stay away from her."

"Yes. But why? Is she evil?" She questions again.

"Lord knows. Though yes, she gives us magical soil to grow our crops and holy water that cures the diseases of our people."

"Then why do people tell us to stay away from her? Grandma?"

"Didn't the elder granny tell you? She takes away girls who are disobedient to their fathers."

"But what if I listen to Father always? And do what he wants? What if I don't question things anymore? Can I talk to her then?"

"No! Never!" Her grandmother yells, furious, "Be cautious. Even if she talks to you nicely, stay away from her. Do not talk!"

"Why?"

"It's obvious, child. She is a woman. A woman who knows too much."

And that - is the only reason she's left with to sleep. The only reason for decades of discrimination, hatred and scalding accusations that woman has faced.

Knowledge.

Months pass, and Anoma watches the time flowing in a repetitive cycle of day and night, of leaves wilting and of sun burning.

One day, she gathers enough courage to tread to the fields surrounding the shrine again. Careful and watching. Peeking over the tall grasses, steps quiet and wary.

"I didn't expect you to return again, young one."

The voice ingrained somewhere in the back of Anoma's head is instantly recognisable.

She yelps out loudly and falls on her butt, groaning slightly. Raising her head seems like a blunder because the woman is staring right back at her. But after her last encounter with the woman, she noticed that her aura never had even a hint of malice. The only fear was the one rooting deep inside her conscience, nurtured since childhood to be wary of this woman of myths.

"I'm sorry." Anoma stood up, fisting the skirt of her tunic, eyes darting here and there. "I just wanted to see the pretty butterfly again."

"Oh. That's unfortunate, I believe they have left."

Anoma looks up but the woman is not looking at her. Her head is tilted to the side, towards the large fields.

"They left? The butterflies?"

"Yes, child. The seasons have changed. They might have flown away to a warmer place."

"Oh, okay."

The disappointment seeps through her voice and then she stands there awkwardly, hoping that the woman would just leave like the last time. Before the conversation could proceed, a large raindrop slaps Anoma on the forehead.

"Ah! It's raining!" She mutters in awe.

"Yes, it is." The woman extends her other hand, palm upwards, the one which did not hold her staff, letting the rain hit.

"The prayers villagers did worked! The gods are making it rain!"

Anoma laughs, glad that a week long ritual that almost every adult in the village participates, was successful in pleasing the rain gods.

"No. The gods don't make rain."

And suddenly, the conversation among adults wondering if the shrine was even dedicated to their gods makes sense. This woman, did she doubt their gods?

Unacceptable!

Angry and desperate to defend the beliefs she was raised with, Anoma questions indignantly.

"Why would you say something like that?"

Suddenly, she's thrown off guard by the slight upward quirk of the woman's lips.

She was smiling.

Anoma realised in horror. The woman could smile!

"Would you like to know how the rain falls?"

Anoma nods dumbly, still perturbed by the current turn of events.

Years later, Anoma learns what happens to the little girls who are disobedient to their fathers. The woman who knows too much takes them by hand and guides them to a world on the other side of the forest.

A world larger than she'd ever imagined. A world of bright colours and books. A world of knowledge. A world where asking questions gives you smiles, not scowls.

A world where women stand equal to men.

A world from her dreams.

The lady smiles at her amazement. "You never know too much." She says, her fingers gently carding through Anoma's hair.

"There is always a world beyond what you see. Always. So learn and grow, little one. Because knowledge is freedom."

The Woman President

By Afreen Shanavas

I always dreamed big. Big enough to be the scapegoat of wet blankets from society, relatives, friends, and pessimists. For long, I remained oblivious of the reason. Later on, I got to know. It was only obvious. My dream was considered paradoxical to my standards. For a woman, it was only a double disincentive. A woman being a leader would be the queerest thing you would hear. That's how it was in my village.

I had always wanted to be a leader. Always. From marshaling the girls in my village to school to escorting the neighbor's sheep, I always had the urge to rule. The only bound my joy knew the day I was selected as the class leader was the fact that this would last only for twenty-nine days. A new student would take

the throne next month. Leaders change. Quite difficult to accept for a bubbling enthusiastic girl often, who wanted to boss people around.

I wailed out of my Mom' womb on November 8, 1905. It was a weird confrontation, honestly. Neither of us knew what to do with the other. The world was confused with me and I was troubled by the notion of being delivered to this strange—what is it called? World?

The battle began then. And to this day, I haven't stopped fighting. Some call me a warrior, but I knew life too well to become friends with it.

Now, what is life? A different day. We've got more pressing issues. To meet our demands, Dad sold matchsticks, toiled in the landlord's field, and shepherded the neighbor's cows while Mom was a domestic help for the same landlord. Amidst the struggle to win bread, they never ignored the simple

pleasures of life, whether it's watching us grow, joining in our scuffles, or playing with us. I was sent to school at the age of five and to this day I consider it an honor. Not all the girls in our village attended school. The first emulation of sexism in my life.

But not the worst.

Life was difficult. With the Great Depression, matters only exacerbated. My brothers and I had to drop out from school. The future was uncertain as ever. The light at the end of the tunnel seemed only a fantasy. A pacifier.

It was on such a day, that I was struck with the harsh reality of life.

I waited on the doorstep, watching the seconds

dissolving to minutes and the minutes dissolving to hours. Occasionally, Mom, in a flurry of movement appeared behind me, peering out into the dark, over my huddled self. Little did I know the wait was in vain. His death did nothing to ameliorate our situation, but the fact that it was somehow my fault, shattered my insides.

Some weeks ago, I had publicly castigated a man twice my age for trying to grope me. That day, I realized he was a ruffian of the most feared bandit in my village. They had their revenge. Only on a different person. But they knew it would crush my insides. Fearing for our safety, Mom packed us out of the

village to another.

The thug's message was crystal clear. I'm not to be meddled with. I have the cart-Blanche to do whatever I wish. In which case, you retaliate, there will be consequences.

Over the next year, the Great Depression alleviated, but my depression level reached an all-time high. All my desires degraded to dreams. The one you see when you sleep.

Now, when I think about it, I realized that those were the moments that stimulated me, empowered me, pulled me from the ground, from out of the shadows to the light, and finally to the most coveted house in American History.

I am what I am because of my Dad, who never gave a damn about what the society thought and my Mom, who always strived until the very last to pay for not only my brother's college but also my education without reluctance. She was never the one to believe that education was useless for girls. On the contrary,

she advocated for equal rights for women, equal pay, and treatment in workplaces to the extent she was murdered by blatant misogynists.

I am left with a world, trying to bury women and muzzle them. I remember learning democratic: Everyone has a voice in decision-making. Do they?

Three years back, I was appointed the Goodwill Ambassador of UNICEF. Easily, it was one of my most treasured moments. Standing at the podium, beaming at the audience, I traced back my path to where it all began. A mixture of emotions lurched through me; pain, for the fact that the people who laid the bricks for my path were not able to witness what their hard work had wrought, happiness, confusion, nervousness, and gratitude. Thinking of what led to this moment; What was the driving force? Where did it all start? There is only one plausible answer.

After high school, I decided to take up work along with my college. I discussed this idea with my brother who suggested that there was a vacancy for a dorm assistant at Emory Dorms, where he was working as one, ad interim.

Without a doubt, I secured the job, juggling a job, and a degree. On the 30th day after my induction to the post, I was quite disappointed. I was paid less than half of what my brother did. Dialing my brother, I wondered out loud at the idiosyncrasy.

"That's how things are, Aloha"

I was thunderstruck at the reply. Okay, I didn't grow up in a village which was brimming with gender equality, but at least I expected to be paid equally for the same work. This incident aroused me. I had had enough.

From being appointed as the President of the City Club to becoming a senator, I had unwavering support from a source which soon after was cut off; My mother.

Her death left an indelible blemish on my life. I was shattered. To this day, I wonder: What was her mistake? Why was she killed?

After her death, I viewed people with disgust; it made me rethink. Why am I working for these people who are not ready to accept the truth? But then I realized, there were always people like that. There never was, is, and will be an ideal country. Perhaps in movies, yes, but not in reality. Still, I had to work for those people who are forced to believe magnificent lies, hindered from seeing the truth and those with no choice except lies.

My designation as the Secretary of State coincided with the untimely death of my-----

"What would you like to drink, Sir?", the stewardess beamed.

The man looked up from My Life, My Story: An Autobiography.

"No, I'm fine, thanks", he waved, summoning a

smile.

"Your Mom's book, I see", she walked off, glancing at the cover.

Hugh nodded at her, looking out at the clouds disappearing behind him. Having dozed off, he roused to the blare of the television.

"Aloha Broughton, President of the United States, who was seriously ill for the past two days has passed away. The cause, as of now is unknown."

Modern Day Feminism

By Udita Mukherjee

She couldn't believe her luck, she would be interviewing the person she had looked up to for three months now. Luck had nothing to do with it, it was biology. Her seniors would say they had picked her for this because she had carefully followed this activist and knew the most about her work revolving around feminism. It only helped that her articles were always meticulous and lucid. Behind closed doors, they would admit they had picked her because she was a woman, just like the interviewee who had quite recently made headlines and garnered national attention. Neither they nor she would ever attribute it to her dedication and hard work. The former because they thought they were doing her a favour, the latter because that is how she had been brought up.

"Annie, she has left her room, we have eyes on her. Prepare, in 3, 2, 1…"

Annie straightened her back, picked up her pen and smiled towards the approaching figure, full of awe.

A bespectacled woman in her late twenties, wearing a loose cotton kurta, breezed in. Her name was Pragati Vikas, a testament to her parents being staunch supporters of progress. Her first sentence acknowledged the interviewer: "You want to know how I became an activist, for that I will have to start at the beginning. My parents taught me to say I am Indian, before anything else. To show I was raised perfectly. Hindu, Muslim, Sikh, Parsi, Christian, Jewish, Cumberbitch, that is all secondary." Annie had yet to ask a question but she already had her first answer and she was impressed. "I have closely followed your work for three months, ma'am. I admire all that you stand for. Would you like to tell me about your background and how it influenced you to become the person you are today?"

"Thank you. I love running into fans and talking to them so this should be fun. To answer your question, my parents always wanted what was best for their only child. So they sent me to an 'all girls school,' to ensure I could become a feminist," Pragati said very matter-of-factly. Annie wondered if she had heard it wrong and thanked her stars she had turned on the recorder. Without a pause, Pragati continued about how she educated herself and spread the ideals of feminism amongst her peers. This led to a few parents complaining she was possessed by the devil. This was when the parents realised they had confused feminist with feminine but they were modern and on top of that they were people of their words, so they took this in their stride. Theirs wasn't a family of quitters. To show their support for their child, they took her to watch a feminist movie they had watched last weekend - Kapoor and Sons. She didn't understand how a movie about men could be feminist. Her parents argued, 'Where do you think Kapoor got his sons from? His wife.' She was sceptical before and after watching the movie. The parents explained - 'You saw how powerfully, unapologetically and without permission she took away the younger son's story and gave it to the elder one? Feminism!' Thus, with her parents' support she resumed feminism with even more gusto. More parents called and complained, even demanded an exorcism. Her parents then had to come up with a more progressive solution - another movie. An English one so that she never made the same mistake as them, never got confused between two words. This time it would be a movie to get her mind off of the feminist obsession and channel that energy into some other issue of concern, like the environment. 'Who wouldn't appreciate a girl who loved to garden?' Time for Forrest Gump – 'that had to be about the environment right? It's in the name.' What she learnt from that experience was to run away as fast as possible whenever any talk of environmental degradation came up - to avoid its serious consequences. A few years passed, Pragati Vikas turned 18. The proper age for sex education. The parents were liberal. They had heard Western schools used videos for this. It was movie time! An English movie, but with Indian values - The 40 year old Virgin. Right from the first scene, the father was forced to reread the morning paper several times and the mother had to start knitting a sweater till the last scene out of sheer modesty, but hey, they didn't back out, they finished the movie. Pragati found the movie informative, to say the least. The lesson was clear – 'Be modern, marry late, most importantly: no sex before 40.' After this incident, they felt they had corrupted their daughter's innocence. How to fix it? An animated movie - Hotel Transylvania! 'Who knows, maybe it would be like a 90 minute course on hotel management, how attractive!' What an essentially Indian and probably Asian way to think! Pragati loved the movie with its cast of vampires, zombies, mummies and other monsters. The parents found it rubbish, very unrealistic. The entire movie was a feat of imagination and creativity so of course they thought it would mess with their kid's mind, make her crazy. Being modern Indians, they couldn't risk the girl's mental health like that. It was time for the last movie, the final showdown, the movie to fix it all, inculcate in the daughter the sense to put herself before others – 'secret to a healthy mind.' They sat down to watch Me Before You. Lesson – 'If you really love someone, you let them go.' It had a great impact on Pragati, influenced her in the way and to the extent her parents did. Oh, how she loved her parents! She concluded by saying: "So I left them, I had to, out of true love. I ran away from home, as fast as possible, to live in Hotel Tenacious which is run by tree-hugging feminists. My kind of people. They guarantee I will remain a virgin till 40, maybe more, my parents are going to be so proud of me!"

Annie burst out laughing. When Pragati didn't join in, she abruptly stopped. "Oh, you were not being sarcastic?"

"Why, what did you think was funny about my answer?" Pragati actually looked clueless.

Annie did not know how to react. First, she hadn't been able to believe her luck, now her ears took a turn at betraying her belief. She kept thinking how a few moments ago she had said she admired Pragati's work. Could she continue to do that after this interview? Maybe Pragati was a feminist but her notions and motivations were very messed up, misguided. She was the perfect example of a person who had been brainwashed by parents who thought they were open-minded and weren't above manipulating the media to prove their point. Annie was amused despite herself at how important issues like feminism, environmental conservation and mental health can be manipulated into a twisted version of what an essentially orthodox set of parents thinks them to mean, to benefit their sense of traditions. She smiled wryly, wondered if she could write this interview as a satire.

"I'm sorry, is the interview over?"

Annie found herself nodding. She got up as Pragati left the room. As a journalist, she had known and even seen that there are all kinds of people. However, after that day's events, she realised there were all kinds of feminists too. It was a mildly depressing and highly discouraging thought. What could a person do? How would one find out if a person was doing the right thing for the wrong reasons? Did it even matter? She picked up her pen, she would write this article, change was slow in coming but maybe it would occur for the right reasons, one interview at a time.

Saving Grace

By Manher Kaur

Grace wiped the plate with the thin-ragged cloth. She looked dully at her reflection in the immaculate glass. Tears depart her eyes, making her cheeks turn blood red. A lump in her neck battled her to work any further. It lost.

When the dishes were through, Grace started scrubbing the coffee table. She urged her eyes to keep open. Energy escaped her body. Fatigue was screaming at her to stop. It lost.

As soon as she recognized the clatter of her husband parking his motorcycle, she hurriedly brushed off the blemishes from the table and stood up attentively. The wicked being entered through the long-standing dull door. He set aside his empty bottles he held onto on the coffee table. Started limping towards his bedroom. "What happened to your leg?" Grace asked, looking down at the floor.

"I tripped," he cleared his throat, "Give me a fresh

pair of clothes." He ordered and disappeared into the darkroom. Grace followed his instructions and fulfilled his command. Afterwards, Grace took out the mop and wiped the muddy footprints he left behind.

The cold-blooded beast entered again, "It is the 2nd day of the month. Which means you must have gotten your salary today, right?"

Grace nodded timidly. "Where have you kept the money?" he asked with a sore throat. "Um, it is somewhere safe."

"The money will be safe with me. Give them to me."

Grace used the word she never believed she could, "No"

"What did you just say to me?" The merciless man raised his voice and rolled up the sleeves of his shirt. His tightened eyes kept glaring at Grace's shattered face.

"No," She replied at the top of her voice. "I know you will use all my money for your vodka and cigarettes and god knows what else you feed on. I work my ass off for this money, so maybe someday we get out of this rotten place you call a 'house'."

"Keep your mouth shut, you whore!" He screamed loud enough to enter the snoring neighbor's houses.

"No, not today." Grace gathered one of his bottles and smashed it on the table. The glass table shattered into pieces at once. He could not recognize those protruding eyes of her. The burning feeling in her chest made her head straight for the dingy floor.

The wicked man grabbed her by the neck and started beating her pitilessly. Her cries and roars went in one ear of the snoring neighbor's and out the other.

Another week flew away, the bruises and bashes almost healed. The pain subsided, yet the lump in the neck remained. The man of the house slept from when the sun rose in the east till it set in the west. While the delicate lady worked every day. Grace wore multiple layers of garments for the week to hide her wounds, since they were not to be met by another soul.

Grace wiped the wet plate with the thin, ragged cloth as she held the plate in her hands and brought it closer to her face. She grimaced at her reflection in the gleaming silver plate with puffy eyes. She wondered, why am I? Why do I exist? Tears rolled down her cheeks, aching the swollen lump under her eyelids.

As soon as her drunkard husband entered through the scruffy wooden door holding an empty bottle in his hand and yelling his head off, Grace jumped in fear. She turned off the faucet and ran out of the kitchen and into the living room. He puts his arm around Grace's shoulders. Her body ached from head to toe, yet she puts her drunk husband to bed. She makes his slumberous body fall on the bed, took off his reeking clothes, and put on warm, fresh ones. Even in a drowsy state, he ordered her to get a clean pair of socks. Grace followed, removed the muddy socks off the boozer's feet, and put on new ones. As she pulled the socks up his toe, he uttered a piercing cry, "That toe is bruised!"

Her heart raced as she glanced at his distended toe. Her heart pounded and her breath grew faster. "Forgive me, please." She looked into his distressed eyes and braced herself as she perceived the subsequent episode. He grabbed her by her hair; her knees bumped against the foot of the bed. He gathered the flower vase from the bedside and smashes it brutally on her back. She cries and wails, begged her vicious husband to have mercy on her. Except he does not.

As the sun shined radiantly in the sky the next morning. Grace woke up, saw to the daily household chores. Packed her husband lunch, iron his clothes and prepared his daily tea. She let out a sigh of relief as he left the house.

Wasted no time on a Sunday, cleaned their tiny shabby apartment. The guests from her book club arrived and entered through the same door her husband let himself out.

Grace's well-behaved friends had a ball discussing more of their neighbor's torrid affair rather than about 'to kill a mockingbird', but Grace felt normal. The pain of her last night's beating subsided and her spirit elevated. Hope clawed it is way back into her life.

It did not last forever. At midnight, she smiled at

the reflection of herself until her husband called out her name.

"Yes?"

"Why are these garments lying crumpled on the floor? They ought to be folded and placed in the closet."

"I was rather occupied today. It will be positively done by tomorrow."

She made her way into the kitchen once again; she smelled something smoky coming from outside. Her face turns red as soon as she entered the living room. The rummy held a bottle of vodka and lighter in his hands above the burning heap of clothes. "I hope you never disobey me again. Clean this after." He walked away.

She forced her wobbly legs to walk towards the stack of clothes and threw herself into the hearth to feel the warmth and affection she longed for.

Doused

By Sharda Mishra

A s I walked past the house in the street of a small village in India, I was startled, and with extreme concerns I asked a man, "Why is all that hubbub and screaming coming from that house?"

"The Mukhiya (Village head) set his daughter-in-law on fire for dowry!" the man said frantically without stopping.

"How can the Mukhiya do that, isn't he supposed to extinguish such practices, rather than setting his own daughter-in-law ablaze on fire?" I expressed my anger.

But I knew empty rhetoric would do nothing.

I have to take action.

I went inside the house and saw the most heart wrenching sight. A woman, in her twenties, was rolling on the ground. The ground was muddy and not paved at all. Surrounding the open courtyard were rooms, kitchen and toilet. On one side was a hand pump with cement plastered all around. There were two jute cots in a corner. As the woman was rolling on the mud to put off the fire it etched marks and scratches on the mud. Her saree was tattered like an old rag by now. Her hair seemed beautifully styled sometime ago.

The newly-wed bride was doused in kerosine oil, her clothes were in flames. She was screaming for help, flailing her arms and legs to put off the fire, while family members were standing and watching. The howling scream was ear splitting. There was not a single woman nearby. It seemed that all the female folks were instructed to stay locked inside the rooms. There were no children either. It looked like a well orchestrated, thoroughly thought-out plan to kill a woman in a bride-dowry case.

As a journalist, I had reported several cases like this and it is one of the saddest truths that still continues even in this day and age. Women are killed for dowry—an age-old deformed tradition which has taken the lives of so many women and will continue to do so.

The moment I stepped in the courtyard, the Mukhiya and his followers became alert.

"Someone hand me a blanket," I almost screamed.

"Fetch me a few buckets of water, quickly."

They suspected that I am a government official. Out of fear, a few men scurried around to find me the things I asked for, while the Mukhiya immediately ran and tried to waylay me at the main entrance to explain himself. But I had turned deaf ears to his explanation. My whole focus was on saving the life of that young woman on fire. The more she moved, the more fuel the flames were getting from the air.

"Move out of my way," I almost pushed the Mukhiya forcefully with disregard.

Without wasting a second, I ran to the woman like the wind. I took my thick scarf and wrapped it around her chest. Just then, I saw a few thick blankets lying on the jute cot. I ran and grabbed them as well. As I was wrapping the woman I saw her whole body was already covered with blisters. Wrapping that blanket around the burning body was not easy, but it was one of those moments when you get the sudden surge of courage and power that leads your path and decision very effortlessly. I wondered, where I got the inner strength and presence of mind to put my anger to action. I was present there; with all my senses awakened, weeping in my heart at another woman burning on fire.

How inhumane this is to treat another human being this way.

The fire was put out after I wrapped her in the blanket, but her body was popping out blisters because of the body heat. I asked all the men to get out of there, and I ripped off the clothes of the young woman and poured buckets of cold water on her—as much as I could. The cold water cooled her down a little, but the moment I stopped pouring water on her, she was back to being steaming hot from inside. I ran outside to get a rickshaw or any vehicle to take the woman to a hospital. Since it was Mukhiya's house I saw lots of Auto rickshaws wandering around. I called one and we set off to the hospital immediately.

My heart was aching. I was glad I could save her life. Before the doctors started any treatment, they wanted to interrogate me first, which I refused vehemently. I was certain that until her treatment started, I wouldn't open my mouth no matter what. I threatened the Mukhiya about the possible consequences and ordered him to use his political power to do whatever he could. The woman had suffered second degree burns, but the doctors assured that she would heal completely.

That night, I stayed in the hospital because I had the feeling that in my absence the Mukhiya would try to kill the woman. After enquiring, I came to know that the woman's husband was not even in the village, instead he was in Punjab working in a carpet factory. The girl was not in a condition to speak with anyone. I called the police station immediately and filed a case against the Mukhiya. There was no paucity of evidence, rather the whole courtyard was strewn with evidence. Cops had no choice but to arrest Mukhiya right away.

The husband was phoned and reported about the mishappenings. He was asked to come home as soon as possible.The woman was still struggling for her life. The pain was unbearable and to see someone go through this was like incessantly going through that same grief and pain. For me it was just disconcerting to be subjected to such an emotional trauma.

I was there to attend my brother's wedding but my whole trip was spent saving the life of that young woman and giving her justice.

"How long will you stay?" my mother asked me.

"I am not leaving until the girl is out of danger—until I feel she is safe," I said firmly. "I am a fervent believer of women empowerment and this incident is completely opposite to my beliefs and ethics."

"Villagers are very stubborn, most won't comply with you against the Mukhiya," my mother warned me.

"I will wait. It doesn't matter how long it takes, but I want to see Mukhiya behind the iron bars serving jail time for the heinous crime he has committed." I was in no mood to let this matter slip into a political drama.

Mukhiya was already arrested. Court hearing started within ten days. All evidence was against Mukhiya. He was imprisoned for twenty-five years without bail.

Within a month the young woman recovered fifty percent. She was heartbroken but happy that she was alive.

"Thank you so much for saving my life." Her words were a gift to me. I would not wish this pain and agony even for my enemy.

The plight of Indian women tied up with these harmful traditions is a real curse for our society.

Eighty Eight

By Uma Fenton

I always sat on a heavy, antique wooden bookshelf, wanting to be written on. I've had different pens accompanying me too, but no, she didn't start writing with me. A frizzy haired girl had received me, a diary, as a gift on her birthday. I call her Friz. She hardly used me when she was young. She was often quiet and alone in her small room. I'd watch her all day.

She was ten years old when one day she came in sobbing. A man entered the room and comforted her, "Stop crying, dear."

"I want mother," she cried bitterly in his arms. "Why did she have to die, daddy?"

Both hugged each other and cried for a long time. Her siblings had also come and cried along with her.

What a tragedy. Perhaps she will write how she

felt about her mother. I remained untouched for a while.

Friz would often sit and read. She read until late evening. Years went by.

One day she came into the room shouting at the top of her voice, "Why not!"

"You know why. Because we're women." said her sister.

"Women?! So what does gender have to do with us wanting to study in the university?"

"The law doesn't allow it. We would be criminals, technically speaking, if we were to request to study there."

"Ridiculous."

The sisters discussed how unfair it was for them not having the opportunity to opt for higher studies only because they were women. For me, on the other hand, I was amazed by how humans differentiated among humans. If only we books had a voice we'd be sharing and lived in awe all the time.

"We have other options," assured her sister.

"If it's not university I'm not opting for anything."

"Father can hardly run the house with what he earns. And with what little he has it is impossible for him to even enrol brother in the university."

"I know." Friz was dejected.

"If you don't continue teaching we won't have anything to eat. It's not like we don't have an option."

"I don't want to be a failure."

"You won't. You won a gold medal at 15, became a teacher at 16, and now on your way to becoming a governess! I wouldn't call that failure."

"Yeah, they've been generous to appoint me as governess. I still think they took pity on us."

"Oh, don't you beat yourself up. Father is in their good books. Just think about it. You earn, pay for my education. Then I return the favor, and we both will have an education."

"Alright, free university it is then."

Friz compromised. Her sister smiled and left the room. Friz then looked towards the shelf and wanted to reach for something. I hope she'd pick me. But now, she took another book and sat there reading. When will she begin to write in me?

I hadn't woken up to a sunrise as beautiful as this. Where am I? The sky was lit up with pinkish orange hues. Absolutely serene. I looked around. What is this? I wasn't placed on that old shelf anymore. I was dusted and relocated. This certainly doesn't look like the place I used to be. I can hear people talking in a different language here. Wow. Friz moved to a different place and brought me along! Maybe she's travelling and will write her travel stories in me. Umm, or maybe about that boy she was talking to her sister about. Oh, I couldn't wait for her to begin her journey with me.

I saw Friz late that night. Looks like she was here to study something. Whatever it is, she had loads of books around the room. Ah, more of reading now! And no writing.

Months passed by, she left me unopened. I think I have to start accepting she carries me around because of sentimental value.

Days passed. I saw her giggling after a really long time. There was a boy who came in often who studied together. They even kissed. Eventually, they got married and moved. I was still moving along with her other belongings.

Every day they did some sort of experiments and they write things down. Friz would too.

Suddenly I saw an angry Friz again, but this time with her husband.

"What does knowledge have to do with gender?"

"I know dear, but it's the rules. Women can't talk."

"We both worked on it. We both need to talk

about it. A speech is a speech, whether voiced by male or female. What does it have to do with me being a woman? Knowledge doesn't discriminate! It can come to anyone and pass through anyone."

"Calm down," he consoled her, "You could give your own speeches, you know."

"Who will listen to them?"

"Well, you can write them down."

"Who will care to read?"

She said that and left the room. I saw her packing their suitcases through the gap of the door. She looked unhappy. Apparently, they were leaving for another country on work.

Years later they both had little girls. She often held them saying, "Never let anyone tell you you're incapable because you are girls."

More days passed. She was lonely. Her husband had died. She now became a single parent to two young children. She was lonely. Although that didn't stop her from doing what she loved best. She read. And I figured out she even took her husband's place at work after his death.

"First woman to hold the position." I heard her tell this to a friend over tea one day.

She also shared how difficult it was for her to do what she wanted to since she was a woman. But she never stopped working hard.

"I am the first woman to win this prize!" she exclaimed.

What an extraordinary woman, I thought. And finally, she took me out of the shelf one day and wrote her first words… or rather numbers. 88.

This is an imagined story of Madam Mari Currie, the frizzy haired girl, who fought against all odds in life to become the greatest woman in science. Poverty, discrimination, law, motherhood, nothing stopped her from being an achiever. The story is written from the perspective of one of her diaries. She was the first woman to become a faculty member of the University of Paris, the first woman to win a Nobel prize. The first person to win Nobel prize in two different fields. She discovered Radium with Atomic Number 88.
PS: Her diary and other personal belongings are still radioactive and are stored in lead-lined boxes.

Subtle Sexism

By Snehal Amembal

What I'm going to talk about isn't obvious. It's far from it. It's subtle. In fact it's so subtle that you may not even have noticed it. Perhaps because you've learned to live with it or maybe because it's so systemic you've come to accept it as the norm. I'm referring to subtle sexism. Sexism that pervades our everyday lives. A kind of sexism that's so difficult to identify yet as women we survive it's malicious web.

It begins very early on. As children we are socialised to accept and imbibe gender roles. With roles, come expectations and it is this mental load of expectations that women have to battle and survive all the time. These expectations then form the very basis of subtle sexism.

Let me try and explain how these expectations are manifested in an everyday setting of our daily existence - At Home.

The woman is often expected to carry out and/ or manage all domestic duties within the home. Again, seeds of these expectations are sowed early on where little girls are encouraged to participate more in house hold chores whilst they see their brothers getting away with it most of the time. As wives and mothers, we are expected to naturally take over the running of the kitchen and chores in general and when the men help it's applauded. They are also immensely thanked for their help. So many times I've seen women unable to live away from their homes even for a few days because the men can't manage on their own. I must admit however that this is slowly changing for the better.

I recently read a quote which said that when a man is doing housework he is simply doing the chores in his house, he is not helping his partner or wife. It made so much sense and very cleverly called out the patriarchy.

The mental load that women experience is at its peak at home. It involves everything to do with keeping track of grocery stock to dental appointments. Somehow, the man comes to view the woman as the "manager" of the household and will participate only upon receiving "instructions" rather than using some good old initiative that his partner or wife is obviously expected to take.

Women are also expected to be agreeable and conforming at all times. I abhor the word "obedient". We are cognitive humans, not animals. Being agreeable leads to being pushed into social networking and maintaining relationships e.g. a daughter-in-law is expected to always be present at family events at her in law's place but is the same always expected from a son in law? I personally know of a few friends who are holding on to unhappy jobs only because they can "escape" from these expectations once in a while. 'Once in a while' because of course they are expected to take leave from work more often than not to fulfil these social obligations.

When a child cries the mother is expected to leave her meal and rush to pacify it. Completely understand if it's feeding related but I've experienced this pattern continuing well past the child turning two years of age! Also, I was horrified to learn that some fathers refuse to change their kid(s)' nappies and some oblige by agreeing to change only wet ones. God forbid the nappy be soiled, the mother is promptly summoned (obviously). Another casual statement that drives me up the wall is about how the father can babysit when the mother is away. It is NOT babysitting when it's your own child. It's parenting! (Louder for those at the back).

Women eating after men at home as well as during family functions/events is another form of subtle sexism. I have never understood this and what infuriates me is that women themselves propagate and reinforce this practice. Younger women are just expected to follow suit except of course if they happen to be pregnant.

Surviving subtle sexism is not easy because one needs to have the courage to firstly identify it and to then challenge it. I must confess here that I've always challenged these so called acceptable ways of living life. I remember even as a child I would feel terrible to see my mum slogging away in the kitchen during festivals and invariably be one of the last ones to eat.

In adolescence, i became more intolerant of these subtle displays of sexism all around me. I was sometimes labelled as 'disrespectful' at other times 'too forward' and at still other times 'downright difficult'. A well meaning (of course) relative once advised my mother to enrol me for an anger management course! The gall!

At work, I was surprisingly popular because of my inherent need to be fair in my dealings and as an HR professional, I was thankfully in a position of influence. Did I mention the popularity didn't permeate through to the management? They did not like being told about gender pay disparities, lack of adequate maternity leave policies and so on. (Read subtle sexism in its best avatar yet!)

Calling out the patriarchal mindset has been enlightening because so many times I find myself in the minority. The "karna padta hai yaar" attitude that some of my peers have adopted is disappointing. When I ask them why, they say they want to keep the peace. At whose expense though?

And this breaks my heart. You are dimming the light of a young woman's life just to uphold some ridiculous patriarchal norms? Where is the sense in all this? How can something you have no control over I.e. your gender end up paving your life's path?

Today, I'm a mother to two very young boys. I want them to grow up without any sense of entitlement because of their gender. The other day, my older son wanted to buy pink coloured flip flops with a unicorn design. I ensured I bought it for him and that he wore it with absolute joy. I also bought my toddler sons a toy kitchen and I actively engage them in household chores from tidying up to loading the washing machine and helping with sorting and even chopping vegetables where possible. I want to ensure that they both become independent young men who will not take it for granted that a woman will "look after" or "pick up after" them.

Subtle sexism is everywhere and the sooner we call it out the better. It's definitely easier said than done but then has anything worth achieving been bereft of difficulty and challenge?!

Parallel

By Sneha Acharekar

A drop of Sun stirred in my cup of tea
A hint of Moonlight and some coffee
A mild shower on a sunny day
A faded orange winter-morning ray
A rainy day spent just indoor
and a rainy day drenched, outdoor
A shining star that stands apart
A moment when a beat skips in the heart
A chirpy morning that is bright
A silent night that seems just right
A touch of shiver running down the back
A long and warm hug with some love-knack
A longing that burns across two hoping hearts
A ride to nowhere, in fairytale horse carts
A fondness floats in, about the way I look
A magical happiness flowing like a brook
That glide on my mind, these are just few...
Whenever I find myself thinking about you.

Aditya read the poem for the nth time and smiled as he looked at his phone. He lay stretched on the bed in his bedroom. The magic of the faded night had not faded from his mind. His mind kept swaying back and forth to the incidences of the previous night. He typed back into his phone and awaited her response restlessly - I can't believe you wrote that for me.

Ohkk. What do you not believe? That 'I' wrote it; or that I wrote it for 'you'?

Aditya smiled to himself and struggled to respond as his phone slipped out of his sleepy grip.

I don't doubt 'you' wrote it. I love you Shamika.

Me too, baby. I can't believe you came at 2 a.m. just to meet me, yesterday. I mean I was so angry initially about whatever happened, but I'm so glad now that it happened. Everything happens for a good reason! See? I told you...

Aditya could not disagree. Everything suddenly seemed to have fallen in place. A few hours ago, a few moments spent together and a few words exchanged; had created magic in their lives. A failed plan of a night out with friends had brought to them an opportunity to spend time with only each other. A severe headache had wasted the whole of the previous day for him. When Shamika had sent him a text to confirm their night-out plan, he had been in two minds about it. With a heavy heart he had responded to her with - *"Sorry, can't make it. I'm down with a terrible headache"* - just an hour prior to the time they had decided to meet up.

Aditya had expected a bit of concern to reflect in Shamika's next message, but he was disappointed when his phone beeped and he read her response - *"That's great. Akash is not responding to my calls. Jennifer is not in the mood to get out of her house. Tripti is making excuses that we meet up tomorrow, instead. And you have a headache! So why am I even here at the venue, already!? This is so awesome!"*

Aditya dialled her number immediately but she did not respond. He then drifted off to sleep for an hour or two. When he woke up, he felt better than before and made another attempt to contact Shamika - no response.

His phone beeped after some time and he read her message across the screen of his phone - *"I'm sorry. You had a headache, but you still responded to my message. The others are not even answering my call. Was I the only one who wanted this plan to work out? I lied at home and so had to leave for somewhere... couldn't stay back at home. Last minute changes don't go well at my place. Hope you feeling better now. Take care."*

Aditya looked up at the clock on his room's wall. It was 11:20 p.m. He felt concerned and texted back -*Where are you?*

Outside.

Okay. He wasn't satisfied with that answer but he let a few minutes pass before he sent her another text. *Where are you, Shamika? I am worried. If it is okay with you, I am feeling better now and we could still meet.* He waited patiently for her response. His phone beeped again after three seemingly long minutes.

It's okay, Aditya. I am out with another friend who wasn't so busy or unwell. We are drinking.

Aditya felt a warm gush of blood run up his spine. After a few minutes of anger however, he felt more concerned, nullified his anger as unreasonable and typed another text message - *Who is this another friend? What are you drinking?*

Shamika did not respond for a few minutes. Aditya began to get restless. He almost counted the 900 odd seconds after which he heard the next text message beep and light up his phone's screen - *Can we still meet up? I can't go home until morning - I'm too drunk... Nihar has to go home, though.*

Aditya did not think before he replied - *Yes, we can. Can you think of an excuse that I can make up at home, right now? Quick!*

Lol. Adi, I am too drunk for an excuse to cook up in my mind right now.

Okay. Give me a few minutes and I will get back to you.

The next few minutes crawled like hours before Aditya had reached the spot where they had decided to meet. When she had reached, he saw her get out of the auto rickshaw calmly and wave at him. He opened the door of his car for her and she threw herself on the seat next to him heavily. Aditya smiled at her, "Vodka?"

"How sweet of you to come at this hour for me, Adi!" Her speech was slurry.

"How many did you drink, Shamika?" He continued to smile.

"I think 3 large. They had a Buy-2-Get-1 free offer... No, I think 4. Buy 2 get 2. And Nihar doesn't drink Vodka. He was having beer."

"Who is Nihar?"

"He's a good friend. Know him since years now. And he's just a friend, okay! His girlfriend was also with us for some time."

"Okay, I was just worried."

"Yes, I understood when you sent me those messages asking for my whereabouts." Shamika looked into his eyes and he saw a mischievous glint in her eyes. "I can't believe you came for me at this hour." She said and threw her head loosely onto the seat's headrest.

"Are you okay? Do you need some water?"

Shamika nodded her head sleepily. She looked into his eyes again and whispered in a sheepish grin, "Thanks for coming." She turned a little louder as she garbled, "I can't imagine wherrre I would have gone like this... drunkkkk, at this hourrr."

"He was so caring. Everything seemed so perfect when we started dating. He would treat me like a princess. I wonder what has got into him." Shamika wept into her phone.

"Has he hurt you physically?" asked Ajay.

"No. He just keeps hurting himself. He starts with an argument and then there's no end to it. He wants more time with me - but he's not even willing to speak with our parents about marriage right now. The arguments are mostly so pointless - they have no head or tail to them. He resorts to emotional blackmail whenever I talk about breaking up!"

Just a few months into her relationship with Aditya, Shamika was reaching the breaking point. The man who she thought was her Prince Charming, had turned life into a nightmare for her. The verbal abuse had become so unbearable that she had lost all respect for him and fallen out of love. She kept going back and forth about her decision to break up with Aditya and thinking about giving their relationship another chance as Aditya continued to end up in tears after every fight, professing his love to her.

Amidst a nasty fight one day, Aditya had suddenly announced to her about a romantic getaway that he had planned for them to a resort, a few miles away from the city. Shamika had no say in the decision as that was his plan for his birthday - saying anything against it would have resulted in yet another fight. She just knew she had to make sure she got herself drunk enough through the evening and drift off to sleep - and that was exactly what she did.

When her eyes opened next, she scanned the room for Aditya but did not find him anywhere. She got up instantly and walked out of the room. The resort was unnaturally silent, notwithstanding a distant chirruping of the insects. Shamika walked out of the room, the resort and towards the parking lot. The dreary sounds of the night were rather loud now. Aditya's car was at the same place where he had parked it in the afternoon. She looked around the place but did not see anyone. Just then she heard the rustling of leaves on her right and her attention shifted towards the shrubs that further ran into a denser jungle. Something about the insipid darkness of the night, pulled her towards the forest. She began to walk ahead, her heart thumping loudly as she felt concerned about Aditya's sudden disappearance. She felt certain he was somewhere in those woods and soon she was walking deeper into the woods.

The droning of the cicadas was getting louder with every step ahead. If the owls still hooted, they were too faint to reach her ears anymore. The light of the moon was not quite reaching her path now as the woods kept getting denser. She wanted to stop right there, but the force kept pulling her further. The sound of her foot steps however, kept her going; even as the path turned stark. The sounds were thankfully, still familiar; as dried twigs snapped under her feet just the way they had initially when she had left from the resort and started to walk towards the jungle.

Her next foot-step however changed this feeling as she felt the dampness of the foliage under her feet. A cold shiver ran down her back as her nostrils sensed the stale scent of blood all around her. In a snap, she felt a hand pull her by the leg and she went thud, on her face - hitting the ground and adding some of her own blood, to the muck. She wanted to scream but she could barely lift she face up. The darkness around grew darker and her eyelids gave in to the heaviness. The senses in her ears however, began to turn clearer with every passing minute. A soft puff of breeze brushed against her ear, and she heard her name in the whisper louder now - "Shamika!"

She opened her eyes with great efforts, only to watch a ghastly face staring back at her; just a breath away. She pushed the face away with all her might and let out a full-throated scream.

"Shhh! Shamika! Why are you screaming?" Aditya sat beside her, dismayed. Shamika wiped the sweat beads off her forehead. "You came here to sleep, is it?" Aditya kissed her on the cheek and began to make further advances.

"Adi, please! I'm not in for this right now." Shamika pleaded.

"When are you ever in for it anymore?" Aditya scowled.

"Is this all you want out of this relationship, Adi?" Shamika wailed and another heated argument followed.

∞ ∞ ∞

"It's like I'm living those nightmares in this parallel. He loves to create drama out of every petty thing."

Aditya had almost begun to stalk Shamika. The more she tried to avoid him, the more he would try to contact her. Soon enough it started to affect her professionally. Aditya began to create scenes outside her workplace; making it quite embarrassing for Shamika to deal with his tantrums. Upon speaking with friends and recognizing the fact that she was at the receiving end of an emotionally abusive relationship; she had decided to seek professional help.

"So what's stopping you from putting an end to this relationship?" Ajay, the counselor on the phone asked.

"He threatens to hurt himself if I do that. It's so scary. He keeps texting that he is cutting his palm... banging his head on the wall... the other day he said he will walk down the railway track and..."

"From whatever I have heard so far, I doubt he would do that - have you seen any of his bruises, ever?" Ajay asked.

"Exactly! Never." Shamika responded instantly.

"You know it already, Shamika. Don't stay victimized like this. Block him from contacting you on every channel. Keep in touch with us and we will guide you further, but you have to trust us completely and follow what we discuss."

Shamika stood firm on her decision to help herself out of the mess she had got into. Sometimes, freedom is just a few dedicated sessions away.

A New Beginning

By Gowri Bhargav

"**D**on't worry. If it turns out to be a girl child, a few drops of juice extracted from this leaf mixed with milk can do the trick," said the notorious Muniamma to Velu and Selvi.

"What's the price?" asked Velu.

"Ten thousand," she said with a sinister smile.

"Don't worry. I'll give you fifteen thousand to bury the secret. We'll just say that she died soon after her birth."

Muniamma was more than happy with the deal. She nodded her head with great delight as she nonchalantly spit the beeda that she had been chewing for quite some time.

"Let me know once your wife develops labor pain. I will come immediately. The midwife is known to me. If the baby delivered is female then I need to act quick before anyone comes to know about our plan."

"Sure, be prepared to receive my call soon. The due date is nearing."

The couple came back to their house. Ponni, their daughter came running to hug Selvi.

"Amma, look what I made when you were away. I made a baby rattle out of palm leaves and tamarind seeds. I wish to gift it to my sister when she is born. I've been praying God everyday that only a girl should be born," exclaimed Ponni innocently.

"Stop Ponni! Don't you dare dream that such a thing should happen. We need a boy. A girl is a liability. She will drain all our wealth. What use is a girl to us? We cannot afford to have another girl," said Velu with great anger.

Ponni recoiled in horror. She was just a nine year old girl. She always wondered why her father had hated her. And now she knew the answer. Her father hated her because she was a girl. With tear laden eyes she hugged her mother.

"Amma! Why is Appa behaving in this manner? I haven't done anything wrong. I want to make him proud someday. And what's wrong in wanting to have a sister?"

It was heart wrenching for Selvi to see Ponni crying. She loved her very much and did not mind having another daughter. But she did not have the courage to voice her opinion for a second time. The first time, with great difficulty she had managed to convince Velu to let Ponni live.

"Don't worry dear. Appa loves you very much. He's just under a lot of tension since his business suffered a heavy loss last month. Now sleep well," she said as Ponni rested on her lap.

Selvi had a sleepless night. A thousand thoughts were hovering in her mind. How could she live with the guilt of killing a girl child? She tossed and turned several times in the bed. And then she had a dream....

In her dream she saw an infant girl smiling innocently at her. She stroked her face with her tender fingers. And then suddenly she wailed in a helpless tone. She was being fed milk mixed with the poisonous extract in a paaladai*. In a few minutes she choked and turned blue. A lifeless infant lay in Selvi's lap.

Selvi woke up in horror. Though it was a dream it seemed like a vision to the impending doom. She couldn't let this happen to her child and had to do something really quick. She thought for some time and came up with a plan. After packing few necessary things she wrote a letter to her husband and tucked it under his pillow. She woke Ponni and asked her to remain quiet. She decided to flee along with Ponni to Chennai.

A few months back an NGO organization "Save Girl Child" had come to their village to create awareness about female infanticide and the right ways to nurture a girl child. Selvi had the opportunity to meet Girija , a volunteer in that organization. Girija had asked her to contact her in case of any suspicious happenings. Selvi had not contacted her all these days because she did not want her husband to get exposed. But she could not remain quiet anymore. She made a frantic call to Girija -

"Girija madam, this is Selvi. It is an emergency. Can I come to Chennai tomorrow and meet you?"

"Oh Selvi! What happened? No problem. Do come. Whatever it is, I will try to help you," said Girija.

"Ma, Where are we going?" questioned Ponni.

"Shh! Don't utter a single word. Just come along with me," she said.

They walked almost a km to reach the nearby bus stop. She knew that a bus heading to Chennai would make a stop at 12 a.m. there. They boarded the bus. She prayed God that she shouldn't get into labor while travelling. Fortunately her prayers were answered and she safely reached Chennai.

Selvi took an auto and finally reached Girija's house. Girija welcomed Selvi and Ponni. Before Girija could ask her anything she burst into tears and started narrating everything. Girija asked her not to worry. She also told her that they could stay with her until suitable arrangements were made for her stay in an ashram. In the meantime Selvi went into labor. She was rushed to the nearby hospital where she delivered a healthy girl child.

∞ ∞ ∞

Velu woke up in the morning and was shocked to

find Selvi and Ponni missing. However he found a letter written by Selvi. She had requested him to change his mindless behavior and also warned him that if he tried to do anything reckless then she would make sure he's put behind bars with the support of the NGO organization. Velu's face turned red. He crumpled the letter and immediately ran to catch the next bus to Chennai.

"How can Selvi do this? It's time I teach her a lesson," he kept telling himself fuming with anger.

In a disoriented manner as he was about to cross the road to reach to the bus stop, he did not notice a speeding truck. In a flash of a moment he felt a sharp pain and he lost his consciousness.

Velu was completely oblivious to everything happening around him. He could hear some muffled voices. It seemed like an operation theatre. Finally after six days he regained his consciousness. Ms Kani , the ER doctor came to check his vitals.

"Mr Velu ! Hope you are doing well now. You met with an accident. A group of college girls spotted you on the road and admitted you in the hospital. You had suffered major injuries but we were able to save you since you were brought here at the right time. Fortunately the nurse whose blood group matched with yours, willingly donated blood to make up for the blood you lost. We are a great team of woman warriors in this hospital. Our only mission is to save lives."

Velu was left speechless. He hung his head in shame.

"A team of women warriors ! All these women have saved my life. And I was going to commit the most heinous crime. I am such an ignominious beast. I have to meet Selvi and Ponni to apologize for my mindless behavior. I pledge to take all necessary efforts to prevent female infanticide."

Velu was discharged from the hospital after a few days. He rushed to Chennai to meet Selvi. Velu broke into tears as soon as he met Selvi. He narrated the incident that had transformed him. He hugged Ponni and was delighted to hold the infant girl.

"My daughters are my greatest wealth," he proudly said.

Selvi was extremely happy upon hearing this. A new beginning awaited the family. Selvi and Velu joined the NGO as volunteers. They attended several workshops and worked relentlessly to spread awareness about the eradication of female infanticide in their village as well as the surrounding rural areas.

Glossary

Paaladai – A cup like utensil with a narrow tip

used traditionally to feed babies.

Wedding after 50

By Ishani Majmundar

Ananya had separated 15 years ago, breaking all knots, from the abusive relationship. She had moved with her little daughter, Samaira at her parents' place. Life wasn't easy but it was still better than before. Her father was a pensioner and day by day with increasing expenses of school and medical, they faced financial crunch so Ananya had decided to resume her career.

One day, it was her birthday and Ananya was in Joggers Park for her morning walk. Her friend had called and so she relaxed on the bench nearby to continue her talk. She was not at all excited about her birthday rather was more tensed about securing a well-paid job. She was discussing her problems. It was then, that a young man, Rohan overheard her. Rohan was doing warm up exercises besides the bench where Ananya was seated. After her phone disconnected, Rohan approached her, "Hey, Rohan Malhotra. I am sorry to overhear your conversation. Don't take me wrong, I am actually Co-Founder of a Stock Broking Firm and also in need of a sincere employee. See, if the job profile suits you, it could be of your help."

He offered his visiting card and asked her to appear for an interview. Ananya was first not convinced but looking at the visiting card, she realised he actually owned the firm.

"Hello Sir, Ananya Sharma. I am really thankful for your kind gesture. I can come for the interview tomorrow." Ananya assured. It was a hope for Ananya to secure the good job.

"That's great Miss Ananya. See you tomorrow at 10 AM sharp. Oh yes, Wish you a very Happy Birthday. And on more thing, please call me just Rohan. Good day."

"Thank you, Rohan, sure I'll reach on time, Good day to you too."

Ananya was impressed by his simplicity but securing the job was the need of the hour. So, she prevented her mind from diverting on other sides. She was able to crack all the interview rounds and secured the job. That job offer was a precious birthday gift for Ananya. And since then, she was working in his firm. Ananya was the oldest employee of his firm, whose hard work had major contribution in the success that Rohan had achieved.

They were more of a family now than friends. Rohan always stood by her whenever she needed any help. Both of their families knew one another well. Samaira could also get along with him quite well. Everything was well from both ends. Both of them liked one another but none of them expressed.

Ananya's daughter Samaira was moving to US for higher studies. She was worried about Ananya, and was sceptical about leaving her alone. She knew that Ananya liked Rohan but would never confess. She many a times tried to explain her, "Ma, why don't you get marry again?"

"Are you crazy Sami? What will our society say? It is your age to get marry beta, I am already above 50 now. Who will marry me at this age?"

"Ma, what if there is someone who loves you and proposes? Will you deny? Love knows no age."

"But, it does create an outrage. You focus on your studies, don't worry about me."

Every time the conversation ended like this. Samaira decided to know the views of Rohan and find out whether he loved Ananya or not. She made up a plan.

One day, Samaira told Ananya that she wanted someone special to meet her. So Ananya presumed it could be Samaira's boyfriend. Hence, she requested Rohan to accompany her to meet the young man. She was a doting mother but at the same time wanted to make sure that Samaira must have chosen the right person. They decided to meet at Jogger's Park. It was Ananya's birthday. Rohan reached before time. His eyes were glued at the gate, waiting for Ananya. After a while, he saw Ananya entering the park. She looked beautiful and gracious, like a Diva. A magical radiance was seen around her. She was actually a Diva. Simple yet elegant peach coloured dress made her look like fairy. Her innocent eyes had a magic. A tight hair updo and few grey strands falling on her shoulder added more beauty. There were wrinkles seen on her face but her sharp jawlines covered them. She never tried to hide the sign of aging and gracefully carried it. The smile she wore was her most precious ornament. Ananya indeed looked stunning at this age.

On another side, Rohan looked very handsome in pair of white shirt and navy blue formal trousers. He looked dashing with his French beard though it was partially grey. It represented his maturity. His body was strong and sturdy even at this age. Rohan's face had started showing few lines, but those were the signs of maturity not ageing, which made him look more handsome. Those grey hair in his beard spoke of his experience gained over years. His inner beautiful soul was shining through his eyes which had never disappointed Ananya.

Rohan's heartbeat skipped when Ananya reached in front of him. He was awestruck. Never in his life he had imagined that he would get to experience such lovely feelings.

There was a mystical aura around. Ananya felt she falling for him. She had never felt so before. There was some magical spell felt that day, as if some miracle was awaiting.

"You look beautiful today Ananya. I cannot take off my eyes." Ananya literally blushed, "Thanks Rohan."

Rohan went on his knees with rose in his hand, "Wishing you a very Happy birthday, a beautiful rose for the beautiful lady in front of me." Ananya was surprised, as she had never expected such a sweet gesture from Rohan.

As Ananya picked the rose, Rohan took out the diamond ring, "Ananya, I couldn't say this before, may I ask your consent to grow old with you? Ananya, I love you, I really do. I am sorry for expressing rather confessing it so late. Shall we spend our remaining lives together? What do you think?" Rohan said it all at once. It was a straight forward proposal and yet romantic in its way. The feelings were pure and natural. Not like young love birds, who feel butterflies in stomach. He was clear and sure.

Ananya was pleased to see that a man, usually with few words, expressed his feelings so beautifully. Rohan's eyes sparkled with deep love and confidence. Depth of his eyes said it all. His voice was deep with honest and serious tone. His smile was gentle as ever. He was a real gentleman, noble and honest always. Ananya had always liked his traits.

Ananya was lost for few moments. She was overwhelmed. She couldn't help but blush more. She had never felt so special before. Never had anyone proposed her or made her feel so special, not even her ex-husband. She had least expected this at this age, that too from Rohan.

Rohan knew everything about her, and how she had managed to walkout and overcome that abusive wedlock, for Samaira's better future. She had spent her entire life raising Samaira well and never had given a second thought about remarrying, rather she was not able to forget her bad past. This was one reason, that Rohan never proposed her before, thinking she might deny.

Ananya was pleased actually. She wished it should not be a dream. She couldn't speak for few seconds, it was so unexpected, but she was more than happy, she gathered the words "Rohan, oh my God, can't believe you are proposing this way. I too have feelings for you since quite long." She took a pause, "You know how everything had been with me so, so I never expressed. I love you too." Her eyes were moist with tears of joy. Ananya accepted the proposal, "We shall, but what about this society, will they accept all this? What will they think? What will Samaira think?"

"I am proposing, after knowing Samaira's consent. So don't worry. Samaira has already approved our relationship."

Ananya asked wiping the moist corner."What?" To which Rohan replied, "Yes, we already had this talk. I never expressed my feelings because I feared you would deny being mother of daughter and society's pressure. I never wanted to lose you and was happy being friends as well. When Samaira told me that you too have feelings for me, I couldn't resist then."

Meanwhile, Ananya's phone buzzed.

Samaira had texted, "Congratulations both of you. I am so glad to see you both together. Mom, hope you liked your someone special. Your table is booked at Water Crest Restaurant. Enjoy your evening. See you both later at night. Love you loads."

"My baby she is such a big girl now. How?" Ananya still couldn't believe that it was all Samaira's plan to bring them together.

"Our baby is indeed a big girl now." Rohan clarified. They both smiled.

They headed towards the restaurant to celebrate the evening. It was a double celebration. It was Ananya's best birthday ever. A week after, they tied the knot in a hush-hush ceremony with few close friends and relatives invited. Thus, they lived happily ever after, with a vow to be with each other till eternity.

One may need to accept the Love the way it is. One must accept, the significant other the way he/she is, with all flaws. Acceptance is needed not compromise. Wedding after 50 is also possible, finding love after 50 is also possible. One needs to clear and sure and not to bother much of the society in front of self and family's happiness.

Wedding After 50

Ananya had separated 15 years ago, breaking all knots, from the abusive relationship. She had moved with her little daughter, Samaira at her parents' place. Life wasn't easy but it was still better than before. Her father was a pensioner and day by day with increasing expenses of school and medical, they faced financial crunch so Ananya had decided to resume her career.

One day, it was her birthday and Ananya was in Joggers Park for her morning walk. Her friend had called and so she relaxed on the bench nearby to continue her talk. She was not at all excited about her birthday rather was more tensed about securing a well-paid job. She was discussing her problems. It was then, that a young man, Rohan overheard her. Rohan was doing warm up exercises besides the bench where Ananya was seated. After her phone disconnected, Rohan approached her, "Hey, Rohan Malhotra. I am sorry to overhear your conversation. Don't take me wrong, I am actually Co-Founder of a Stock Broking Firm and also in need of a sincere employee. See, if the job profile suits you, it could be of your help."

He offered his visiting card and asked her to appear for an interview. Ananya was first not convinced but looking at the visiting card, she realised he actually owned the firm.

"Hello Sir, Ananya Sharma. I am really thankful for your kind gesture. I can come for the interview tomorrow." Ananya assured. It was a hope for Ananya to secure the good job.

"That's great Miss Ananya. See you tomorrow at 10 AM sharp. Oh yes, Wish you a very Happy Birthday. And on more thing, please call me just Rohan. Good day."

"Thank you, Rohan, sure I'll reach on time, Good day to you too."

Ananya was impressed by his simplicity but securing the job was the need of the hour. So, she prevented her mind from diverting on other sides. She was able to crack all the interview rounds and secured the job. That job offer was a precious birthday gift for Ananya. And since then, she was working in his firm. Ananya was the oldest employee of his firm, whose hard work had major contribution in the success that Rohan had achieved.

They were more of a family now than friends. Rohan always stood by her whenever she needed any help. Both of their families knew one another well. Samaira could also get along with him quite well. Everything was well from both ends. Both of them liked one another but none of them expressed.

Ananya's daughter Samaira was moving to US for higher studies. She was worried about Ananya, and was sceptical about leaving her alone. She knew that Ananya liked Rohan but would never confess. She many a times tried to explain her, "Ma, why don't you get marry again?"

"Are you crazy Sami? What will our society say? It is your age to get marry beta, I am already above

50 now. Who will marry me at this age?"

"Ma, what if there is someone who loves you and proposes? Will you deny? Love knows no age."

"But, it does create an outrage. You focus on your studies, don't worry about me."

Every time the conversation ended like this. Samaira decided to know the views of Rohan and find out whether he loved Ananya or not. She made up a plan.

One day, Samaira told Ananya that she wanted someone special to meet her. So Ananya presumed it could be Samaira's boyfriend. Hence, she requested Rohan to accompany her to meet the young man. She was a doting mother but at the same time wanted to make sure that Samaira must have chosen the right person. They decided to meet at Jogger's Park. It was Ananya's birthday. Rohan reached before time. His eyes were glued at the gate, waiting for Ananya. After a while, he saw Ananya entering the park. She looked beautiful and gracious, like a Diva. A magical radiance was seen around her. She was actually a Diva. Simple yet elegant peach coloured dress made her look like fairy. Her innocent eyes had a magic. A tight hair updo and few grey strands falling on her shoulder added more beauty. There were wrinkles seen on her face but her sharp jawlines covered them. She never tried to hide the sign of aging and gracefully carried it. The smile she wore was her most precious ornament. Ananya indeed looked stunning at this age.

On another side, Rohan looked very handsome in pair of white shirt and navy blue formal trousers. He looked dashing with his French beard though it was partially grey. It represented his maturity. His body was strong and sturdy even at this age. Rohan's face had started showing few lines, but those were the signs of maturity not ageing, which made him look more handsome. Those grey hair in his beard spoke of his experience gained over years. His inner beautiful soul was shining through his eyes which had never disappointed Ananya.

Rohan's heartbeat skipped when Ananya reached in front of him. He was awestruck. Never in his life he had imagined that he would get to experience such lovely feelings.

There was a mystical aura around. Ananya felt she falling for him. She had never felt so before. There was some magical spell felt that day, as if some miracle was awaiting.

"You look beautiful today Ananya. I cannot take off my eyes." Ananya literally blushed, "Thanks Rohan."

Rohan went on his knees with rose in his hand, "Wishing you a very Happy birthday, a beautiful rose for the beautiful lady in front of me." Ananya was surprised, as she had never expected such a sweet gesture from Rohan.

As Ananya picked the rose, Rohan took out the diamond ring, "Ananya, I couldn't say this before, may I ask your consent to grow old with you?

Ananya, I love you, I really do. I am sorry for expressing rather confessing it so late. Shall we spend our remaining lives together? What do you think?" Rohan said it all at once. It was a straight forward proposal and yet romantic in its way. The feelings were pure and natural. Not like young love birds, who feel butterflies in stomach. He was clear and sure.

Ananya was pleased to see that a man, usually with few words, expressed his feelings so beautifully. Rohan's eyes sparkled with deep love and confidence. Depth of his eyes said it all. His voice was deep with honest and serious tone. His smile was gentle as ever. He was a real gentleman, noble and honest always. Ananya had always liked his traits.

Ananya was lost for few moments. She was overwhelmed. She couldn't help but blush more. She had never felt so special before. Never had anyone proposed her or made her feel so special, not even her ex-husband. She had least expected this at this age, that too from Rohan.

Rohan knew everything about her, and how she had managed to walkout and overcome that abusive wedlock, for Samaira's better future. She had spent her entire life raising Samaira well and never had given a second thought about remarrying, rather she was not able to forget her bad past. This was one reason, that Rohan never proposed her before, thinking she might deny.

Ananya was pleased actually. She wished it should

not be a dream. She couldn't speak for few seconds, it was so unexpected, but she was more than happy, she gathered the words "Rohan, oh my God, can't believe you are proposing this way. I too have feelings for you since quite long." She took a pause, "You know how everything had been with me so, so I never expressed. I love you too." Her eyes were moist with tears of joy. Ananya accepted the proposal, "We shall, but what about this society, will they accept all this? What will they think? What will Samaira think?"

"I am proposing, after knowing Samaira's consent. So don't worry. Samaira has already approved our relationship."

Ananya asked wiping the moist corner."What?" To which Rohan replied, "Yes, we already had this talk. I never expressed my feelings because I feared you would deny being mother of daughter and society's pressure. I never wanted to lose you and was happy being friends as well. When Samaira told me that you too have feelings for me, I couldn't resist then."

Meanwhile, Ananya's phone buzzed.

Samaira had texted, "Congratulations both of you. I am so glad to see you both together. Mom, hope you liked your someone special. Your table is booked at Water Crest Restaurant. Enjoy your evening. See you both later at night. Love you loads."

"My baby she is such a big girl now. How?" Ananya still couldn't believe that it was all Samaira's plan to bring them together.

"Our baby is indeed a big girl now." Rohan clarified. They both smiled.

They headed towards the restaurant to celebrate the evening. It was a double celebration. It was Ananya's best birthday ever. A week after, they tied the knot in a hush-hush ceremony with few close friends and relatives invited. Thus, they lived happily ever after, with a vow to be with each other till eternity.

One may need to accept the Love the way it is. One must accept, the significant other the way he/she is, with all flaws. Acceptance is needed not compromise. Wedding after 50 is also possible, finding love after 50 is also possible. One needs to clear and sure and not to bother much of the society in front of self and family's happiness.

The Perennial Colourful Thread

By Alipi Das

It is not one short story, but a collection of short stories united by a single familiar thread. In our childhood, we loved to listen to the fairy tales that our grandmas narrated to us. It always ended, And the prince and the princess lived happily ever after. It concluded with a blissful ending, and the child in us slept peacefully, dreaming of the fairyland and the happy life; ever after. Did the real-world ever be that one lucky, charming fairyland? From the grandmas' times to the present day, did anything change drastically? Let us find out.

By the way, let me introduce myself; I am a freelance writer searching for plots to develop my fiction, and the moment I look around, I squeal, "Oh! It is everywhere; I need to scratch the surface to visualize the naked truth."

∞∞∞

Tani is a qualified professional but an introvert. Her parents are desperately trying to fix an appropriate alliance for her.

"Your daughter is too thin; hope her health is fine," asks a son's mother.

Another one says, "Apply turmeric paste regularly before a bath; your face will glow."

The suggestions follow.

"Our boy is too tall. You have to wear heels when you go out with him."

"What can you cook? My son loves different cuisines."

"Do you want to work after marriage? How will you manage your household responsibilities?"

The most bizarre attitude over the phone, "Shall your daughter; stand out among ten girls in a row?"

And the questions continue.

Tani feels that her job interview is simpler than; the search for her life-partner. She sometimes tries to question herself, "Is there something lacking in me? Am I not a complete woman?" Her mother now and then understands her daughter's dilemma and pacifies her.

Tying Tani's hair, she narrates anecdotes from her times, "Did I ever tell you what happened when alliances started coming in for me? One of them asked me to show my teeth. It seemed; that if someone had gaps between their teeth and were jutting out, it was a symbol of bad luck and ill fate. One of them even asked me to walk, and they checked if only my toes and heels touch the ground or the entire feet, which symbolized the soon-to-be-a-widow."

The search persists, and the predicament of the subdued lady exists.

∞ ∞ ∞

Ruchi, an affable, outgoing girl and a mind of her own, is head over heels in love with Navin. With big plans and starry dreams of their future, they are all set to tie the knot with their respective families' consent and blessings. Her parents accept the demands of the groom's side, from a destination wedding to expensive gifts for the groom's family members, later to find their only daughter fighting a lonely, messy battle of threats, demands, and divorce.

Ruchi answers the phone, "Yes, I am fine. Why did you call me?"

"I just called to talk to you, Ruchi. I am your mother; do I need an excuse to call you? You sound stressed, is something bothering you? Talk to me, please."

Ruchi retorts defiantly, "No, I am busy will talk to you later."

"I have always supported Ruchi in every step of her life. I feel so helpless and dejected to see her in such a condition at the rehabilitation centre. I will always be there for her; whenever she recovers from her alcohol addiction and depression."

Navin's suave attitude bowls everyone; at the initial stages, from her parents, relatives, friends to the treating physicians. It is a matter of time to unveil the root cause of Ruchi's current disorder and Navin's calculated manoeuvres.

Tara's mother goes on warning Chamu, their housemaid, "Beware of your husband's misdeeds. You are toiling hard and earning, and your husband is snatching it away from you and spending on his drinks and other women. Look at the scars on your face and body! Why don't you leave him? How will you manage your work if you take leave often?"

Chamu, in-between her bouts of wailing explains, "Madam, where will I go with my babies? I don't have any place to stay. My sisters live-in far-off villages with their families and struggling to meet ends. My mother lives with my brother's family at the foothills of the mountain. My brother's wife will not allow us to stay; she has her family. I stay in the village on top of the mountain and travel for one hour on foot to come here for work. Please understand, and don't throw me out. I have to take care of my children."

The mobile beeps and interrupts their dialogue, and Tara's mother instructs Chamu to finish off the chores. She lovingly responds, "Dear, I was waiting for your call, w…" she couldn't finish her sentence.

"Mom, I want to tell you something," Tara's voice quivers. She continues, "I cannot take this anymore; it is mental torture. You advise me to put up with him and his frivolous activities, hoping one day your son-in-law will realize and change his habits, but how long do I have to wait? Is your societal status more valuable than my well-being? Why do I have to wear a mask and put up a fake show of happiness and underplay my real-life situation?"

Tara's mother firmly replies, "Patience is what nowadays girls are lacking. Do you know your grandpa had another woman in his life? Your grandma was a strong-willed woman. She did not leave her in-law's house and brought us all up single-handedly. Throughout her life, she never disrespected your grandpa and immediately forgave and accepted him when he came back to her, finally."

"Are you comparing two separate eras on the same podium? I can't believe; you are an educated lady with such an archaic mental set up." Tara disconnects the mobile, eyes burning with rage and tears streaming down her cheeks.

Is there any difference between Chamu and Tara?

Ila goes and sits on the banks of the river, watching the ducks quacking and wading through the mud, the scorching sun's reflection sparkling on the water. She takes a deep breath and hums a tune in oblivion, her only time to indulge in her pastime. Gradually the sun's ochre shadow reclines. Ila jumps up and rushes back home. The time for her relaxation is over.

She thinks, "Is it my home or a prison?"

The mother-in-law and sister-in-law always orders and control the entire environment of the house. One tiny lapse of her responsibilities calls for innumerable bickering and a barrage of profanities. The father-in-law and husband are forever mute spectators, actively watching either the news or sports on TV.

The neighbour's wife visits them in the evening, "My husband got transferred to the city from this suburb. We will be leaving soon. Do come and visit us when you are in the city."

Ila's heart aches, while she nods and thinks, "When did she last meet her parents? She didn't want them to suffer; her plight and pains will aggravate

their tensions and ill health."
She heaves a sigh and continues with her daily activities.

Along the seashore, Gowri accompanies her mother. The scarlet sun setting on the horizon. She stoops to collect the seashells; her mother calls out, "Gowri, walk fast; it is getting late. We have to prepare dinner. Your father will be back soon, and your brother must be feeling hungry."
Reluctantly she picks up the bamboo basket and skips ahead. She loves to play and make beautiful items out of these seashells – birds, butterflies, fishes, vegetables, flowers, fruits, so many of them, all stacked in one of the corners of their little shack.
At home, Gowri eyes her brother, who is busy studying. Assisting her mother in the kitchen for dinner, Gowri asks her, "Ma, why can't I go to school like Ravi?"
Her mother, after a fleeting laugh, replies, "You are a girl. What will you do by going to school? Anyway, once you grow up, you must get married and help your fisherman husband in selling fish in the market. At home, you must manage the kids and household tasks, just like me, so you better learn quickly from my
training."

Her dreams nipped in the bud by her mother; as she plants the root firmly into Gowri's tender brain that marriage is the only goal of a grown-up girl.

The sketches are all analogous. The female species are all unified by the same fate – Marriage and the husband, their only destiny as dictated by society. I must find the core reason of my protagonists' quandary. I ponder for a while, and by my instinct, and will-power plunge deep into their lives to dissect the inner self. My plans are simple. Behind every agony, there is a robust rationale and a way out. I'm the messiah in this direction. My few helpful friends assist me in organizing; a one-to-one meeting with each family, which progresses into ongoing, multiple discussions, henceforth. It wasn't easy, but trials and tribulations have their own victory.

Ila's mother-in-law is easy to convince. "Thank you so much for agreeing to my proposal." I beam at my achievement.

The deal is Ila will do a job offered by me, and part

of her salary is to be set aside for the marriage purposes of her sister-in-law. She couldn't thank me more, her eyes well-up at the prospect of visiting her parents in town; and pursue her singing.

Gowri's parents agree to her attending school if I keep my promise; of bearing the cost of her marriage when she grows up. The little girl dances and giggles; when she hears of joining school. Ila is an art teacher in the same school where Gowri attends. She trains Gowri in singing and hones her skills in articles from seashells. The displays sell in exhibitions and fairs. The money deposited in an account for Gowri's discretion; after she becomes an adult.

Tani accepts the offer; and joins the rehabilitation centre as a psychotherapist; where Ruchi gets admitted.

Every day Tani chats with Ruchi regarding her bright prospects, "None of the challenges thrown to you in your life is big enough to consider it. Just visualize yourself striding into this world-famous university, your feelings when you first step into it. Focus only on your future aspirations now; this very moment will

become a memory of the past."

Both find solace in each other's words and arms; their self-confidence increases with tide and time.

Tara is now occupied in her significant role, managing various projects. She is one of the directors for both; the rehabilitation centre and the school for the destitute. Her minute supervision and managerial skills ensure the smooth functioning of these organizations. She also admits Chamu's tots to the school and provides free food for all children.

The above stories are all widespread; but connected by a single colourful thread, which changes its shade at every intermittent space. All my protagonists relate to one another but continue their lives forward with or without a spouse or partner. The societal travesties outlast, but they all survive with a bold look, a smiling face, an optimistic attitude, a content mindset, and endless grit and determination.

My role is minuscule in this entire small, round world, more like a liaison person. I can correlate with the agonies of my heroines, and; connect the dots and spin the perennial colourful thread of a big family story; for their smooth passage of life from one phase to another. With this, I end my fairy tale in my unique way, "And they lived their lives happily ever after, but on their own terms and conditions."

Bittersweet Chocolate

By Vaishali Chandorkar Chitale

Harshita sat despondently on the chair, sipping her morning cup of tea. The daily bunch of newspapers were lying unopened next to her, on the coffee table. She could see the vast emptiness of her life spread out in front of her. How had things come to this pass, she wondered?

Today, when the world was grappling with Covid 19 pandemic that had everyone in its deadly grip, her services were most needed (she being a microbiologist!), but she was sitting at home, frustrated and straining at the leash to be let loose in her beloved laboratory to research this miniscule coronavirus and find out its genesis. She wanted to join the race for finding the vaccine for this life-threatening infectious disease, but it would mean to rock the marital boat, which was anyway on dangerous waters as it is!

Life had literally been a bed of roses till some

years back. The roses had now wilted and the thorns had begun to prick. When had it started? Was it when she took a step back in her career to pander to her husband's fragile ego or when she deliberately underplayed her achievements for him to shine in the world?

She came from a family of over achievers. Her father, Ashok Pradhan was a leading orthopaedic surgeon in a reputed hospital of the city. Her mother, Uma was a doctorate in 'Human factors and Cognitive Psychology', and had taught post graduates in the University till recent past, now retired. Her brother Dilip and Alka his wife, too were super specialist doctors having their own practice and leading a fulfilling busy life.

How had she lost the plot? Her parents had always drilled into her the importance of a good education and she had done them proud. The talk around the dining table every evening of biology and its various streams had ensured her interest in biological sciences and various organism kept growing. She had done her PhD in Microbiology and was fascinated by the tiny, not visible to the naked eye world of bacteria and viruses. She had authored many papers on effects of these micro-organisms on human body and environment.

True to the family calling, she had married a doctor too. Sameer was a cardiac surgeon of repute and was the last word on congenital heart issues. They had met at a conference on 'Bacteria and its invasion on Heart, held in New Delhi. She had spotted him as soon as she had entered the hall, with his arresting face and commanding presence. Listening to him talk later when he presented his paper was the clincher. She was mesmerized by his boyish charm, the lopsided smile while answering a query and the way he breezed through the presentation in a devil-may-care attitude; in an absolute anti-thesis of what she had imagined a heart surgeon would be!

They had ended up having dinner together on the first night itself, through her carefully contrived machinations. Conversation flowed as smooth as silk. She was happy to learn his views on working women and was further re-assured when he mentioned that his mother, a diabetologist in her own right had supported the family income throughout his growing up years. The cherry on the cake was that he was also from her city, Mumbai. They spent all their free time together during those four days and by the end of the conference, she was as sure as the dawn rising in the east every day, that she had found her soulmate. Till date, she barely remembers anything else of those heavenly days, except going around with a permanent goofy smile on her face and her heart singing a tune of its own.

Things moved fast after that. Families met, a wedding arranged and the nitty grittes settled. Rings exchanged; vows done. They had rented a moderate two bedroom flat, near her parents' house and employed a full day help to do the household chores. Cooking had never been her strong point, so she was happy to see food on the table and thanked her stars that Sameer was not a fussy eater too.

The initial days after marriage had been good fun, both waving good byes after breakfast and meeting around dinner time, tired and happy to see each other again. Sipping a nightcap or two after dinner, discussing the days' work and enjoying each other's company with soft lights and semi classical music playing in the background was something she looked forward to everyday.

So, when had trouble entered their paradise? she ruminated. Was it when her paper on various Influenzas in the world (her first amongst many), had got published in a medical magazine of repute and Sameer had not shown any interest? She had thought that he would be as excited as her and proud of her achievement at so young an age, but his lukewarm response had puzzled her. She hadn't given it another thought then, dismissing it as a one-time incident; attributing it to his long tiring day at the hospital or maybe his upcoming operation next day.

But slowly her perfectly woven tapestry of a happy married life had begun to unravel. As she started making a name for herself in the world of microbiology, Sameer changed from his usual jovial self to being irritated at the most mundane things, like papers not neatly stacked on the table! It was so gradual that she failed to see the signs in the beginning. It was not as if he didn't have a successful career, he too was an upcoming heart surgeon with operations scheduled every day. He worked long hours, his opinion was sought within his peers and he enjoyed professional success. Maybe, given these circumstances, she failed to join the dots at first.

She began to realise that something was amiss when she heard him putting her down very carefully, so as not to sound impolite, at a party when her peers praised her and underplay her achievements. She found her colleagues at many get- togethers on the back foot justifying their opinion about her. She knew she was good in her work and deserved every inch of the merit she got. She loved her work and had been published many times in scientific journals. So, she was at a loss when Sameer brushed off her research work as something that all microbiologists do!

She began to see a pattern. He would come home very late the day she had some news to give. He began avoiding shop talk. The one thing they connected most on was their interest in each other's branch of science and had spent many pleasant evenings discussing their common passion. Now it was a thing of the past. He would closet himself in his study after dinner, ostensibly preparing for the next day and she would spend a listless evening reading or watching TV.

It was difficult to reconcile the Sameer of today with the man she had fallen in love with. She didn't want to believe that he was like the innumerable males out there, envious and insecure of their wives' success. If she could be proud of his achievements, what stopped him from being of hers? What is it about the male ego, which just can't let them accept a woman can do as well, if not better than them in their careers? Why is it that a woman always has to take a back seat and be sensible one of the two?

But she also knew, professional and personal lives have to go hand in hand for a happy and joyful life. If the balance is tipped, life becomes a journey to be endured and not enjoy. She wanted a long innings like her parents and knew it was up to her to save her marriage. How she wished the world had more men like her father and brother who had the generosity of the heart and were secure in their space to accept a woman doing well in her chosen path.

She recalled what she had once read in Grey's Anatomy, "At some point you have to make a decision. Boundaries don't keep other people out. They fence you in. Life is messy. That's how we are made. So, you can waste your lives drawing lines. Or you can live your life crossing them." She knew it was up to her to cross her boundary. It would have been easy to stuck to her guns, but what would it have achieved? Humans are fallible, no one's perfect. She still loved him with all his insecurities and foibles and was ready to take that extra step.

She had saved her marriage, no doubt, but the bitterness hit her more than ever now, thinking about the global crisis. She wanted to be in the fore front in the war against covid. Why does one have to choose in life? Why can't we have it all? Giving up her flourishing career had been her choice; he had never asked her to. Their families though supportive had held their opinion. The elephant in the room was always there, unspoken but visible. As she sat there morosely, thinking of the 'road not taken', Sameer came in.

But today, there was something different about him. He walked up to her, held her gaze and took her hands in his. Tugging at her hands, he made her stand and took her close. Hugging her to him, he gently cupped her face in his hands and softly said, "Harshita, go and conquer the world. You are not meant to sit at home and see the world go by. Live your life and be joyful as your name! If you are not happy, how can I be happy? I married you knowing that you are a committed professional, I can't take that away from you. I am sorry for letting my insecurities get better of me, it will not happen again. I will try my best, it will take time, but it will happen, I promise you with all my heart."

She was stunned to hear that. She looked at him disbelievingly, what had brought this change of heart? Did he really mean it? He gave her a wry look and holding her gaze said," I am so sorry for causing you so much pain. My mother noticed your unhappiness and drilled some sense into me. When we were young, she was never at home when we got back from school. I loved her of course, but something in me also hated the fact that she prioritised her work over us. But then, she reminded me the happy time we spent on her days off. She said she could devote her time completely to us when at home, only because she felt fulfilled as a person. She had a life beyond being a wife and mother. She chided me for being a fool and told me that she had not raised a fool, and not to insult her upbringing." He smiled ruefully and said, "She told me to smarten up my act and get the smile back on your face!"

Hearing his words, a dam burst from her. She clung to him crying and let her tears flow. She felt something poking in her back and turned around. He was holding a brand new PPT kit, which he gave it to her with a flourish reminiscent of their olden days. Smiling up at him, eyes shining with love she gave him a dazzling smile . Now, she knew the man she had fallen in her love with was back and he meant every word he spoke. Her heart was bursting with joy as it reaffirmed her belief that she had chosen wisely and her instincts had not failed her after all.

Her Last Wish

By Anwesha Panda

"I hate you Maa."

"I know but can you please forgive me? People say that they love their mothers the most in the world and you, my baby you hate me? I cannot rectify the mistakes but please try to understand I am dependent on your father and I am bound to do whatever he says.

"Seriously Maa? You think anything you say justifies what you did?"

"I had no option. Which mother would want such a fate? The most precious possession of a mother is her beloved child. But you hate me, and you should. I deserve to be hated."

"Yes, you do. Because it's not 18 th century or something where women don't have any voice. You are a spineless and uneducated person who doesn't even how to take a stand neither for herself nor for her family. My words hurt, right? And your pain is just nothing in comparison to what you did.”

“Things aren't much different today, especially here. The patriarchal society still dominates here. I know I am spineless, uneducated and naive too. I didn't have the courage to stand for my rights back, when my father thought my education is needless or when they wanted me to get married at 16. Do you think it was easy for me? I barely knew anything; I didn't even know that's illegal. My childhood, my dreams, my consent wasn't important. It still isn't. When I complained to my mother, she used to say 'That is how it works. The sooner you used to it, the better for you.' My life's only motive was to be an ideal wife, an ideal daughter in law and of course a good mother. Or so I thought because that is what they made me think. I questioned my existence in this society. WHO AM I? Someone's daughter, someone's wife. Someone's mother? That's all? But as an individual? Who am I and where do I stand in society? I'm nothing...”

“Maa please.”

“No, please let me complete. Don't stop me today. You are the only one to whom I can pour my heart out to... I was expected to bear the child who would carry forward the legacy, even when I wasn't ready to carry it physically or mentally. I was forced upon by your father. I still get shivers down my spine when I think about those nights. Soon I was expecting my first child but things got worse when the doctor said I won't be able to make it through the gestation period because of my weakness and being underweight. So we had to abort. Everything was beyond my imagination and control. They blamed me, saying there must be something wrong with me. But this was just the beginning. There was more to come. My bright days were gone and the forever dark gloomy days set in. I didn't have any say when the beast kept forcing himself upon me.

Then I was expecting you. This time I was really very happy and felt very positive. It all seemed like a dream. I kept talking to you and forgot all my pain. I couldn't wait to meet you..."

"Maa enough, I don't want to listen to all those again. There's no use telling me these because I still hate you and I always will. I'm sorry but I can't forgive you."

Her voice started fading away as I fell asleep. She is the only person in my life whom I genuinely love and I love her the most. But I'm so unfortunate that she won't love me back, Never ever. I wish I had an option. I don't feel good here without her. Though we talk almost every day but I still miss her presence. She says she looks like me but I know she is even more beautiful. The most pious soul and with the most beautiful heart because not a single day of her passes without talking to me. She says she hates me, but I am her mother.

She cannot lie to me. I know deep down she loves me too but she'd never admit that. Tomorrow is her birthday and I will prepare all her favourite dishes. She is not just my daughter, she is my best friend. I'd formed a very strong bond with her right from the beginning. She has my eyes which always speak the truth. And I know she's not as naive as I am. She is fearless, bold and the righteousness and fierceness she has, always makes me think that she is an incarnation of Draupadi. She pretends to be heartless and hides her grief from me, just the way I do...

"What are you doing in the kitchen for so long?" asked my mother in law.

"It's her birthday today. And you know what I do on her birthdays."

"What a shameless person you are? You should be thankful to us that we are still allowing you to stay under this roof. But instead, you're answering me back? You have become insane and just because we don't say anything that doesn't mean..."

I preferred to ignore and stay silent as I know it's useless and she is actually right. But do I have any other option after my parents denied me to stay in their house? Weird rules no, once you're married, your husband's home is your home and not the one where you were born and brought up. But as my mother used to say 'that is how it works here.'

"Maa, you had your lunch?"

"My baby, happy birthday. See what all I made for you!"

"What an irony. You're still celebrating my birthday. I would have turned 17 today only if I was alive."

My heart sinks in whenever she says this. "Why did you say that? I'll give you a tight slap."

"Because you killed me, even before I could see your face."

"My baby please just stop it now. I couldn't do anything. I was unconscious and when I woke up, everything had already ended. I kept on searching for you everywhere and asked for you to everyone. That is when they said to me that you were killed. And my world turned upside down. Do you think I wanted this? No. I loved you more than anyone and I still do. You have my flesh and blood. You are a part of me. You see, they think I'm a psychopath but they can't see you the way I do. They can't see my love for you. Forcefully giving me pills so that I stop seeing you but they don't know that you are the reason I'm still surviving. Please try to understand my pain. You are the only one who can."

I hear her sobs and see her teary eyes as she holds my face in her hands and wipes away my tears. I am well aware that this is my hallucination and she exists now only in my imagination. She always did.

"Maa please don't cry. No matter how much I hate you, I can't see you crying."

"What else can an ill-fated mother like me do? Your father got remarried after knowing my condition. I couldn't take the trauma of losing you. I had no one left to call my own. They let me stay here not because of sympathy but because they were guilty. They are responsible for this condition of mine and I won't ever forgive them just the way you can't forgive me. But sometimes I feel its better that you are not here. What's the point of facing so much hardship? You wouldn't be allowed to study, you'd face creeps and lewd comments the moment you step out, you wouldn't be allowed to wear the clothes of your choice and if you did, they'd call you names. As the mother of a girl child, I'd be having nightmares if you get late while returning. You and I, both would be having a constant fear no matter where we are, be it outside or even at our own home. Even if things are fine, you would be compelled to get married soon and expected to make babies, be a good mother, a good wife and die. Why would I choose such an awful life for you where you have no voice of your own and even if you have, that would be suppressed. Because you know as my mother used to say 'That is how it works here.' And I would never want my princess to live a life that I lived."

"Maa, you're so strong and I am proud of you but why do you sound so gloomy today?"

"Because now I know what I want. I've wanted this for the last 17 years. I have had enough and I can't take it anymore. I want to be with you forever now and fulfil all my duties of being your mother." I could see her face turn pale as she heard what I just said. As I set my foot at the edge of the terrace, She comes closer and says, "Maa no matter what I say, you know that I love you and I always did.

Yes, I still can't forgive you because I think you could've saved me but I still love you. Please don't do this."

This was the first time ever she said this. I've waited ages for this moment. I couldn't help but cry bitterly.

"I've wanted this all this while, to be finally united with you in the other world, but you always tell me to either wait or try to change the topic. But your mother is tired now. You tell me is there any reason for me to be alive?"

I see her standing speechless. She has got no answer to my question. I smile at her and say "Meet you soon" instead of a goodbye because I know I'm going to be with her soon. I close my eyes and take a leap.

∞∞∞

Now we are in a beautiful world of ours. We are happy here. There is no one who would question us. My pretty daughter wears anything she wants to. She stays out for late nights and yet I can sleep peacefully because I know she is safe now. She does whatever she wants and seeing her, I relive my own life. We play like kids and laugh till our stomach hurts. She takes me on long drives.

People are often afraid of death but I wish I'd died earlier instead of staying around the beasts. And in the end, I hope in some other birth, I would be a good mother to my daughter. I want to be somewhere, where I won't have to go through denial to educational, gender discrimination, abuses, harassments, marital rapes and a lot more. Where I won't have to see my daughter getting killed by female infanticide and my husband getting remarried without divorcing me, just because we couldn't have a son. And I wish someday somewhere, we all are safe and I hope it isn't just in my imagination.

Heavy box

By Minakshi

'Your Son has lasted his life for his love.' A man in a well-uniformed dress said to an old lady who seemed to be waiting for someone at the door. He kept a heavy box there in the hall and left with gratitude in their eyes.

That old lady was about to cry but her eyes were filled with pride and satisfaction. She didn't show anything; she went inside and called her daughter-in-law who was about 7-month pregnant. That young girl was so excited because just before two days, his husband had promised to come for her. He went on the mission and after that, they decided to celebrate their anniversary together. He told her that he was bringing a silver anklet for her as a gift. She was eagerly waiting for her husband in a light pink saree with small earrings that matches her color of eye shadow. Her open hair with bold kajal and silver-colored bangles were

waiting for the anklets to decorate her bare legs.

That old lady entered her room and by rubbing her hair softly she said 'My daughter, come with me.'

When Meera Singh saw tears in her mother-in-law's eyes, she asked 'Mom, why are there tears in your eyes?'

'No nothing. Just come with me.' That old lady said whose eyes were not accepting the pain of losing his young son.

Meera excitedly came outside in the hall to see his husband "Late. Tushar Singh". After coming outside, she saw that there was no one except the heavy box. She took the help of a chair to sit down and asked her mom-in-law 'Where is he? He lied to me; he sent gifts instead of coming. I will never talk to me. How could he...'

'Beta, He can't talk now.' Preeti Singh, her mom-in-law said in between her talks.

Meera lifted her face and asked curiously 'What happened? Why are you saying this? Is everything alright? What, speak up Mom?' she was sweating in tension.

'Calm down! My child, please. It is hard to accept but you have to accept the truth that your husband has sacrificed his life for this motherland...'

Without uttering any word, she started opening that box. The first thing, she saw after disclosing the box was the anklet that he promised to gift her. She took it out from that box and tied it in her bare feet. She stood up to go back to her room but

then; after moving four steps she felt dizzy and fainted.

Preeti alleged first but sprinted towards the hospital. Meera got admitted to I.C.U for immediate surgery as her condition was incompetent.

After performing surgery for two hours, finally, the doctor came and said 'I am sorry, your grandson has been born unhealthy. We have to keep him under 24-hour observation. Maybe he will not survive for long. We are trying our best to rescue his life but it seems to be impossible. Remain strong and support your daughter-in-law this time!'

'What?' Mrs.Preeti Singh said in a crying tone and sat on the chair nearby the ward. She was worried about the patient lying inside with closed eyes and disappointing silence on her face. Everything seemed to be blurry and disagreeable. She wanted to scream and cry aloud but she couldn't. It is impossible to measure the emptiness and sorrow inside her. 'What would happen when Meera will come to know about this? She would die after realizing the thing ambulating around.' All this thought was striking in her mind while sitting alone. Preeti moved inside the hospital room and sat beside Meera's bed.

She softly rubbed Meera's head and whispered 'Everything will be alright my daughter. I know that you are strong but you need to be stronger now.'

Meera suddenly started opening her eyes after

hearing the whisper of her Mom. She said in a strong voice and tears in her eyes ' Mom, Why it happened to me? I lost everything. Why? Am I so bad that everything got snatched from me? I know Tushar sacrificed his life for our safety, but how to accept this truth that he will never come again to meet me and our child.' She then asked about his son whose first cry disturbed her ears while being senseless.

'You have to be strong now. I don't want to say that but I have to say it; your child is unhealthy and he would not survive for more than a day or two. I am so sorry to say that but he is still under observation and you would not be able to lift him in your hands until he is alive.'

Meera went into extreme shock. The day she imagined to be lovely and memorable turned into a terrorful dream which she just wanted to forget. She remained silent for a while and then spoke up with a heavy voice 'Mom, will you approve two of my decisions?'

'Yes beta, speak up your wish.' Preeti said.

'Mom, I want to go in defense to protect my motherland. I can't see my son now. I am not courageous enough to lift the pain of losing him again. I can't........ '

'I can understand your pain. Calm down! I am with you in every decision of yours.

After a day, that tiny one-day-born boy died. After resisting herself; Meera went to attend her child's funeral. She saw her child for the first and last

time. She pretended to be strong in front of the other people but when she returned home, she cried aloud. She kept on crying for the whole day. Preeti was consoling her but not stopping her from crying. She lost her husband, son, and grandson but still she was trying to stay strong. At last, her painful silence broke down in tears.

'Mom, I am back. Hug me.' A note with this message came along with the heavy box after two years.

'Your daughter has lasted her life in a bomb blast. Jai hind!'

Heavy box

'Your Son has lasted his life for his love.' A man in a well-uniformed dress said to an old lady who seemed to be waiting for someone at the door. He kept a heavy box there in the hall and left with gratitude in their eyes.

That old lady was about to cry but her eyes were filled with pride and satisfaction. She didn't show anything; she went inside and called her daughter-in-law who was about 7-month pregnant. That young girl was so excited because just before two days, his husband had promised to come for her. He went on the mission and after that, they decided to celebrate their anniversary together. He told her that he was bringing a silver anklet for her as a gift. She was eagerly waiting for her husband in a light pink saree with small earrings that matches her color of eye shadow. Her open hair with bold kajal and silver-colored bangles were

waiting for the anklets to decorate her bare legs.

That old lady entered her room and by rubbing her hair softly she said 'My daughter, come with me.'

When Meera Singh saw tears in her mother-in-law's eyes, she asked 'Mom, why are there tears in your eyes?'

'No nothing. Just come with me.' That old lady said whose eyes were not accepting the pain of losing his young son.

Meera excitedly came outside in the hall to see his husband "Late. Tushar Singh". After coming outside, she saw that there was no one except the heavy box. She took the help of a chair to sit down and asked her mom-in-law 'Where is he? He lied to me; he sent gifts instead of coming. I will never talk to me. How could he...'

'Beta, He can't talk now.' Preeti Singh, her mom-in-law said in between her talks.

Meera lifted her face and asked curiously 'What happened? Why are you saying this? Is everything alright? What, speak up Mom?' she was sweating in tension.

'Calm down! My child, please. It is hard to accept but you have to accept the truth that your husband has sacrificed his life for this motherland...'

Without uttering any word, she started opening that box. The first thing, she saw after disclosing the box was the anklet that he promised to gift her. She took it out from that box and tied it in her bare feet. She stood up to go back to her room but

then; after moving four steps she felt dizzy and fainted.

Preeti alleged first but sprinted towards the hospital. Meera got admitted to I.C.U for immediate surgery as her condition was incompetent.

After performing surgery for two hours, finally, the doctor came and said 'I am sorry, your grandson has been born unhealthy. We have to keep him under 24-hour observation. Maybe he will not survive for long. We are trying our best to rescue his life but it seems to be impossible. Remain strong and support your daughter-in-law this time!'

'What?' Mrs.Preeti Singh said in a crying tone and sat on the chair nearby the ward. She was worried about the patient lying inside with closed eyes and disappointing silence on her face. Everything seemed to be blurry and disagreeable. She wanted to scream and cry aloud but she couldn't. It is impossible to measure the emptiness and sorrow inside her. 'What would happen when Meera will come to know about this? She would die after realizing the thing ambulating around.' All this thought was striking in her mind while sitting alone. Preeti moved inside the hospital room and sat beside Meera's bed.

She softly rubbed Meera's head and whispered 'Everything will be alright my daughter. I know that you are strong but you need to be stronger now.'

Meera suddenly started opening her eyes after

hearing the whisper of her Mom. She said in a strong voice and tears in her eyes ' Mom, Why it happened to me? I lost everything. Why? Am I so bad that everything got snatched from me? I know Tushar sacrificed his life for our safety, but how to accept this truth that he will never come again to meet me and our child.' She then asked about his son whose first cry disturbed her ears while being senseless.

'You have to be strong now. I don't want to say that but I have to say it; your child is unhealthy and he would not survive for more than a day or two. I am so sorry to say that but he is still under observation and you would not be able to lift him in your hands until he is alive.'

Meera went into extreme shock. The day she imagined to be lovely and memorable turned into a terrorful dream which she just wanted to forget. She remained silent for a while and then spoke up with a heavy voice 'Mom, will you approve two of my decisions?'

'Yes beta, speak up your wish.' Preeti said.

'Mom, I want to go in defense to protect my motherland. I can't see my son now. I am not courageous enough to lift the pain of losing him again. I can't........ '

'I can understand your pain. Calm down! I am with you in every decision of yours.

After a day, that tiny one-day-born boy died. After resisting herself; Meera went to attend her child's funeral. She saw her child for the first and last

time. She pretended to be strong in front of the other people but when she returned home, she cried aloud. She kept on crying for the whole day. Preeti was consoling her but not stopping her from crying. She lost her husband, son, and grandson but still she was trying to stay strong. At last, her painful silence broke down in tears.

'Mom, I am back. Hug me.' A note with this message came along with the heavy box after two years.

'Your daughter has lasted her life in a bomb blast. Jai hind!'

Heavy box

'Your Son has lasted his life for his love.' A man in a well-uniformed dress said to an old lady who seemed to be waiting for someone at the door. He kept a heavy box there in the hall and left with gratitude in their eyes.

That old lady was about to cry but her eyes were filled with pride and satisfaction. She didn't show anything; she went inside and called her daughter-in-law who was about 7-month pregnant. That young girl was so excited because just before two days, his husband had promised to come for her. He went on the mission and after that, they decided to celebrate their anniversary together. He told her that he was bringing a silver anklet for her as a gift. She was eagerly waiting for her husband in a light pink saree with small earrings that matches her color of eye shadow. Her open hair with bold kajal and silver-colored bangles were

waiting for the anklets to decorate her bare legs.

That old lady entered her room and by rubbing her hair softly she said 'My daughter, come with me.'

When Meera Singh saw tears in her mother-in-law's eyes, she asked 'Mom, why are there tears in your eyes?'

'No nothing. Just come with me.' That old lady said whose eyes were not accepting the pain of losing his young son.

Meera excitedly came outside in the hall to see his husband "Late. Tushar Singh". After coming outside, she saw that there was no one except the heavy box. She took the help of a chair to sit down and asked her mom-in-law 'Where is he? He lied to me; he sent gifts instead of coming. I will never talk to me. How could he...'

'Beta, He can't talk now.' Preeti Singh, her mom-in-law said in between her talks.

Meera lifted her face and asked curiously 'What happened? Why are you saying this? Is everything alright? What, speak up Mom?' she was sweating in tension.

'Calm down! My child, please. It is hard to accept but you have to accept the truth that your husband has sacrificed his life for this motherland...'

Without uttering any word, she started opening that box. The first thing, she saw after disclosing the box was the anklet that he promised to gift her. She took it out from that box and tied it in her bare feet. She stood up to go back to her room but

then; after moving four steps she felt dizzy and fainted.

Preeti alleged first but sprinted towards the hospital. Meera got admitted to I.C.U for immediate surgery as her condition was incompetent.

After performing surgery for two hours, finally, the doctor came and said 'I am sorry, your grandson has been born unhealthy. We have to keep him under 24-hour observation. Maybe he will not survive for long. We are trying our best to rescue his life but it seems to be impossible. Remain strong and support your daughter-in-law this time!'

'What?' Mrs.Preeti Singh said in a crying tone and sat on the chair nearby the ward. She was worried about the patient lying inside with closed eyes and disappointing silence on her face. Everything seemed to be blurry and disagreeable. She wanted to scream and cry aloud but she couldn't. It is impossible to measure the emptiness and sorrow inside her. 'What would happen when Meera will come to know about this? She would die after realizing the thing ambulating around.' All this thought was striking in her mind while sitting alone. Preeti moved inside the hospital room and sat beside Meera's bed.

She softly rubbed Meera's head and whispered 'Everything will be alright my daughter. I know that you are strong but you need to be stronger now.'

Meera suddenly started opening her eyes after

hearing the whisper of her Mom. She said in a strong voice and tears in her eyes ' Mom, Why it happened to me? I lost everything. Why? Am I so bad that everything got snatched from me? I know Tushar sacrificed his life for our safety, but how to accept this truth that he will never come again to meet me and our child.' She then asked about his son whose first cry disturbed her ears while being senseless.

'You have to be strong now. I don't want to say that but I have to say it; your child is unhealthy and he would not survive for more than a day or two. I am so sorry to say that but he is still under observation and you would not be able to lift him in your hands until he is alive.'

Meera went into extreme shock. The day she imagined to be lovely and memorable turned into a terrorful dream which she just wanted to forget. She remained silent for a while and then spoke up with a heavy voice 'Mom, will you approve two of my decisions?'

'Yes beta, speak up your wish.' Preeti said.

'Mom, I want to go in defense to protect my motherland. I can't see my son now. I am not courageous enough to lift the pain of losing him again. I can't........ '

'I can understand your pain. Calm down! I am with you in every decision of yours.

After a day, that tiny one-day-born boy died. After resisting herself; Meera went to attend her child's funeral. She saw her child for the first and last

time. She pretended to be strong in front of the other people but when she returned home, she cried aloud. She kept on crying for the whole day. Preeti was consoling her but not stopping her from crying. She lost her husband, son, and grandson but still she was trying to stay strong. At last, her painful silence broke down in tears.

'Mom, I am back. Hug me.' A note with this message came along with the heavy box after two years.

'Your daughter has lasted her life in a bomb blast. Jai hind!'

Heavy box

'Your Son has lasted his life for his love.' A man in a well-uniformed dress said to an old lady who seemed to be waiting for someone at the door. He kept a heavy box there in the hall and left with gratitude in their eyes.

That old lady was about to cry but her eyes were filled with pride and satisfaction. She didn't show anything; she went inside and called her daughter-in-law who was about 7-month pregnant. That young girl was so excited because just before two days, his husband had promised to come for her. He went on the mission and after that, they decided to celebrate their anniversary together. He told her that he was bringing a silver anklet for her as a gift. She was eagerly waiting for her husband in a light pink saree with small earrings that matches her color of eye shadow. Her open hair with bold kajal and silver-colored bangles were

waiting for the anklets to decorate her bare legs.

That old lady entered her room and by rubbing her hair softly she said 'My daughter, come with me.'

When Meera Singh saw tears in her mother-in-law's eyes, she asked 'Mom, why are there tears in your eyes?'

'No nothing. Just come with me.' That old lady said whose eyes were not accepting the pain of losing his young son.

Meera excitedly came outside in the hall to see his husband "Late. Tushar Singh". After coming outside, she saw that there was no one except the heavy box. She took the help of a chair to sit down and asked her mom-in-law 'Where is he? He lied to me; he sent gifts instead of coming. I will never talk to me. How could he…'

'Beta, He can't talk now.' Preeti Singh, her mom-in-law said in between her talks.

Meera lifted her face and asked curiously 'What happened? Why are you saying this? Is everything alright? What, speak up Mom?' she was sweating in tension.

'Calm down! My child, please. It is hard to accept but you have to accept the truth that your husband has sacrificed his life for this motherland…'

Without uttering any word, she started opening that box. The first thing, she saw after disclosing the box was the anklet that he promised to gift her. She took it out from that box and tied it in her bare feet. She stood up to go back to her room but

then; after moving four steps she felt dizzy and fainted.

Preeti alleged first but sprinted towards the hospital. Meera got admitted to I.C.U for immediate surgery as her condition was incompetent.

After performing surgery for two hours, finally, the doctor came and said 'I am sorry, your grandson has been born unhealthy. We have to keep him under 24-hour observation. Maybe he will not survive for long. We are trying our best to rescue his life but it seems to be impossible. Remain strong and support your daughter-in-law this time!'

'What?' Mrs.Preeti Singh said in a crying tone and sat on the chair nearby the ward. She was worried about the patient lying inside with closed eyes and disappointing silence on her face. Everything seemed to be blurry and disagreeable. She wanted to scream and cry aloud but she couldn't. It is impossible to measure the emptiness and sorrow inside her. 'What would happen when Meera will come to know about this? She would die after realizing the thing ambulating around.' All this thought was striking in her mind while sitting alone. Preeti moved inside the hospital room and sat beside Meera's bed.

She softly rubbed Meera's head and whispered 'Everything will be alright my daughter. I know that you are strong but you need to be stronger now.'

Meera suddenly started opening her eyes after

hearing the whisper of her Mom. She said in a strong voice and tears in her eyes ' Mom, Why it happened to me? I lost everything. Why? Am I so bad that everything got snatched from me? I know Tushar sacrificed his life for our safety, but how to accept this truth that he will never come again to meet me and our child.' She then asked about his son whose first cry disturbed her ears while being senseless.

'You have to be strong now. I don't want to say that but I have to say it; your child is unhealthy and he would not survive for more than a day or two. I am so sorry to say that but he is still under observation and you would not be able to lift him in your hands until he is alive.'

Meera went into extreme shock. The day she imagined to be lovely and memorable turned into a terrorful dream which she just wanted to forget. She remained silent for a while and then spoke up with a heavy voice 'Mom, will you approve two of my decisions?'

'Yes beta, speak up your wish.' Preeti said.

'Mom, I want to go in defense to protect my motherland. I can't see my son now. I am not courageous enough to lift the pain of losing him again. I can't........ '

'I can understand your pain. Calm down! I am with you in every decision of yours.

After a day, that tiny one-day-born boy died. After resisting herself; Meera went to attend her child's funeral. She saw her child for the first and last

time. She pretended to be strong in front of the other people but when she returned home, she cried aloud. She kept on crying for the whole day. Preeti was consoling her but not stopping her from crying. She lost her husband, son, and grandson but still she was trying to stay strong. At last, her painful silence broke down in tears.

'Mom, I am back. Hug me.' A note with this message came along with the heavy box after two years.

'Your daughter has lasted her life in a bomb blast. Jai hind!'

Heavy box

'Your Son has lasted his life for his love.' A man in a well-uniformed dress said to an old lady who seemed to be waiting for someone at the door. He kept a heavy box there in the hall and left with gratitude in their eyes.

That old lady was about to cry but her eyes were filled with pride and satisfaction. She didn't show anything; she went inside and called her daughter-in-law who was about 7-month pregnant. That young girl was so excited because just before two days, his husband had promised to come for her. He went on the mission and after that, they decided to celebrate their anniversary together. He told her that he was bringing a silver anklet for her as a gift. She was eagerly waiting for her husband in a light pink saree with small earrings that matches her color of eye shadow. Her open hair with bold kajal and silver-colored bangles were

waiting for the anklets to decorate her bare legs.

That old lady entered her room and by rubbing her hair softly she said 'My daughter, come with me.'

When Meera Singh saw tears in her mother-in-law's eyes, she asked 'Mom, why are there tears in your eyes?'

'No nothing. Just come with me.' That old lady said whose eyes were not accepting the pain of losing his young son.

Meera excitedly came outside in the hall to see his husband "Late. Tushar Singh". After coming outside, she saw that there was no one except the heavy box. She took the help of a chair to sit down and asked her mom-in-law 'Where is he? He lied to me; he sent gifts instead of coming. I will never talk to me. How could he...'

'Beta, He can't talk now.' Preeti Singh, her mom-in-law said in between her talks.

Meera lifted her face and asked curiously 'What happened? Why are you saying this? Is everything alright? What, speak up Mom?' she was sweating in tension.

'Calm down! My child, please. It is hard to accept but you have to accept the truth that your husband has sacrificed his life for this motherland...'

Without uttering any word, she started opening that box. The first thing, she saw after disclosing the box was the anklet that he promised to gift her. She took it out from that box and tied it in her bare feet. She stood up to go back to her room but

then; after moving four steps she felt dizzy and fainted.

Preeti alleged first but sprinted towards the hospital. Meera got admitted to I.C.U for immediate surgery as her condition was incompetent.

After performing surgery for two hours, finally, the doctor came and said 'I am sorry, your grandson has been born unhealthy. We have to keep him under 24-hour observation. Maybe he will not survive for long. We are trying our best to rescue his life but it seems to be impossible. Remain strong and support your daughter-in-law this time!'

'What?' Mrs.Preeti Singh said in a crying tone and sat on the chair nearby the ward. She was worried about the patient lying inside with closed eyes and disappointing silence on her face. Everything seemed to be blurry and disagreeable. She wanted to scream and cry aloud but she couldn't. It is impossible to measure the emptiness and sorrow inside her. 'What would happen when Meera will come to know about this? She would die after realizing the thing ambulating around.' All this thought was striking in her mind while sitting alone. Preeti moved inside the hospital room and sat beside Meera's bed.

She softly rubbed Meera's head and whispered 'Everything will be alright my daughter. I know that you are strong but you need to be stronger now.'

Meera suddenly started opening her eyes after

hearing the whisper of her Mom. She said in a strong voice and tears in her eyes ' Mom, Why it happened to me? I lost everything. Why? Am I so bad that everything got snatched from me? I know Tushar sacrificed his life for our safety, but how to accept this truth that he will never come again to meet me and our child.' She then asked about his son whose first cry disturbed her ears while being senseless.

'You have to be strong now. I don't want to say that but I have to say it; your child is unhealthy and he would not survive for more than a day or two. I am so sorry to say that but he is still under observation and you would not be able to lift him in your hands until he is alive.'

Meera went into extreme shock. The day she imagined to be lovely and memorable turned into a terrorful dream which she just wanted to forget. She remained silent for a while and then spoke up with a heavy voice 'Mom, will you approve two of my decisions?'

'Yes beta, speak up your wish.' Preeti said.

'Mom, I want to go in defense to protect my motherland. I can't see my son now. I am not courageous enough to lift the pain of losing him again. I can't........ '

'I can understand your pain. Calm down! I am with you in every decision of yours.

After a day, that tiny one-day-born boy died. After resisting herself; Meera went to attend her child's funeral. She saw her child for the first and last

time. She pretended to be strong in front of the other people but when she returned home, she cried aloud. She kept on crying for the whole day. Preeti was consoling her but not stopping her from crying. She lost her husband, son, and grandson but still she was trying to stay strong. At last, her painful silence broke down in tears.

'Mom, I am back. Hug me.' A note with this message came along with the heavy box after two years.

'Your daughter has lasted her life in a bomb blast. Jai hind!'

Heavy box

'Your Son has lasted his life for his love.' A man in a well-uniformed dress said to an old lady who seemed to be waiting for someone at the door. He kept a heavy box there in the hall and left with gratitude in their eyes.

That old lady was about to cry but her eyes were filled with pride and satisfaction. She didn't show anything; she went inside and called her daughter-in-law who was about 7-month pregnant. That young girl was so excited because just before two days, his husband had promised to come for her. He went on the mission and after that, they decided to celebrate their anniversary together. He told her that he was bringing a silver anklet for her as a gift. She was eagerly waiting for her husband in a light pink saree with small earrings that matches her color of eye shadow. Her open hair with bold kajal and silver-colored bangles were

waiting for the anklets to decorate her bare legs.

That old lady entered her room and by rubbing her hair softly she said 'My daughter, come with me.'

When Meera Singh saw tears in her mother-in-law's eyes, she asked 'Mom, why are there tears in your eyes?'

'No nothing. Just come with me.' That old lady said whose eyes were not accepting the pain of losing his young son.

Meera excitedly came outside in the hall to see his husband "Late. Tushar Singh". After coming outside, she saw that there was no one except the heavy box. She took the help of a chair to sit down and asked her mom-in-law 'Where is he? He lied to me; he sent gifts instead of coming. I will never talk to me. How could he...'

'Beta, He can't talk now.' Preeti Singh, her mom-in-law said in between her talks.

Meera lifted her face and asked curiously 'What happened? Why are you saying this? Is everything alright? What, speak up Mom?' she was sweating in tension.

'Calm down! My child, please. It is hard to accept but you have to accept the truth that your husband has sacrificed his life for this motherland...'

Without uttering any word, she started opening that box. The first thing, she saw after disclosing the box was the anklet that he promised to gift her. She took it out from that box and tied it in her bare feet. She stood up to go back to her room but

then; after moving four steps she felt dizzy and fainted.

Preeti alleged first but sprinted towards the hospital. Meera got admitted to I.C.U for immediate surgery as her condition was incompetent.

After performing surgery for two hours, finally, the doctor came and said 'I am sorry, your grandson has been born unhealthy. We have to keep him under 24-hour observation. Maybe he will not survive for long. We are trying our best to rescue his life but it seems to be impossible. Remain strong and support your daughter-in-law this time!'

'What?' Mrs.Preeti Singh said in a crying tone and sat on the chair nearby the ward. She was worried about the patient lying inside with closed eyes and disappointing silence on her face. Everything seemed to be blurry and disagreeable. She wanted to scream and cry aloud but she couldn't. It is impossible to measure the emptiness and sorrow inside her. 'What would happen when Meera will come to know about this? She would die after realizing the thing ambulating around.' All this thought was striking in her mind while sitting alone. Preeti moved inside the hospital room and sat beside Meera's bed.

She softly rubbed Meera's head and whispered 'Everything will be alright my daughter. I know that you are strong but you need to be stronger now.'

Meera suddenly started opening her eyes after

hearing the whisper of her Mom. She said in a strong voice and tears in her eyes ' Mom, Why it happened to me? I lost everything. Why? Am I so bad that everything got snatched from me? I know Tushar sacrificed his life for our safety, but how to accept this truth that he will never come again to meet me and our child.' She then asked about his son whose first cry disturbed her ears while being senseless.

'You have to be strong now. I don't want to say that but I have to say it; your child is unhealthy and he would not survive for more than a day or two. I am so sorry to say that but he is still under observation and you would not be able to lift him in your hands until he is alive.'

Meera went into extreme shock. The day she imagined to be lovely and memorable turned into a terrorful dream which she just wanted to forget. She remained silent for a while and then spoke up with a heavy voice 'Mom, will you approve two of my decisions?'

'Yes beta, speak up your wish.' Preeti said.

'Mom, I want to go in defense to protect my motherland. I can't see my son now. I am not courageous enough to lift the pain of losing him again. I can't........ '

'I can understand your pain. Calm down! I am with you in every decision of yours.

After a day, that tiny one-day-born boy died. After resisting herself; Meera went to attend her child's funeral. She saw her child for the first and last

time. She pretended to be strong in front of the other people but when she returned home, she cried aloud. She kept on crying for the whole day. Preeti was consoling her but not stopping her from crying. She lost her husband, son, and grandson but still she was trying to stay strong. At last, her painful silence broke down in tears.

'Mom, I am back. Hug me.' A note with this message came along with the heavy box after two years.

'Your daughter has lasted her life in a bomb blast. Jai hind!'

Heavy box

'Your Son has lasted his life for his love.' A man in a well-uniformed dress said to an old lady who seemed to be waiting for someone at the door. He kept a heavy box there in the hall and left with gratitude in their eyes.

That old lady was about to cry but her eyes were filled with pride and satisfaction. She didn't show anything; she went inside and called her daughter-in-law who was about 7-month pregnant. That young girl was so excited because just before two days, his husband had promised to come for her. He went on the mission and after that, they decided to celebrate their anniversary together. He told her that he was bringing a silver anklet for her as a gift. She was eagerly waiting for her husband in a light pink saree with small earrings that matches her color of eye shadow. Her open hair with bold kajal and silver-colored bangles were

waiting for the anklets to decorate her bare legs.

That old lady entered her room and by rubbing her hair softly she said 'My daughter, come with me.'

When Meera Singh saw tears in her mother-in-law's eyes, she asked 'Mom, why are there tears in your eyes?'

'No nothing. Just come with me.' That old lady said whose eyes were not accepting the pain of losing his young son.

Meera excitedly came outside in the hall to see his husband "Late. Tushar Singh". After coming outside, she saw that there was no one except the heavy box. She took the help of a chair to sit down and asked her mom-in-law 'Where is he? He lied to me; he sent gifts instead of coming. I will never talk to me. How could he...'

'Beta, He can't talk now.' Preeti Singh, her mom-in-law said in between her talks.

Meera lifted her face and asked curiously 'What happened? Why are you saying this? Is everything alright? What, speak up Mom?' she was sweating in tension.

'Calm down! My child, please. It is hard to accept but you have to accept the truth that your husband has sacrificed his life for this motherland...'

Without uttering any word, she started opening that box. The first thing, she saw after disclosing the box was the anklet that he promised to gift her. She took it out from that box and tied it in her bare feet. She stood up to go back to her room but

then; after moving four steps she felt dizzy and fainted.

Preeti alleged first but sprinted towards the hospital. Meera got admitted to I.C.U for immediate surgery as her condition was incompetent.

After performing surgery for two hours, finally, the doctor came and said 'I am sorry, your grandson has been born unhealthy. We have to keep him under 24-hour observation. Maybe he will not survive for long. We are trying our best to rescue his life but it seems to be impossible. Remain strong and support your daughter-in-law this time!'

'What?' Mrs.Preeti Singh said in a crying tone and sat on the chair nearby the ward. She was worried about the patient lying inside with closed eyes and disappointing silence on her face. Everything seemed to be blurry and disagreeable. She wanted to scream and cry aloud but she couldn't. It is impossible to measure the emptiness and sorrow inside her. 'What would happen when Meera will come to know about this? She would die after realizing the thing ambulating around.' All this thought was striking in her mind while sitting alone. Preeti moved inside the hospital room and sat beside Meera's bed.

She softly rubbed Meera's head and whispered 'Everything will be alright my daughter. I know that you are strong but you need to be stronger now.'

Meera suddenly started opening her eyes after

hearing the whisper of her Mom. She said in a strong voice and tears in her eyes ' Mom, Why it happened to me? I lost everything. Why? Am I so bad that everything got snatched from me? I know Tushar sacrificed his life for our safety, but how to accept this truth that he will never come again to meet me and our child.' She then asked about his son whose first cry disturbed her ears while being senseless.

'You have to be strong now. I don't want to say that but I have to say it; your child is unhealthy and he would not survive for more than a day or two. I am so sorry to say that but he is still under observation and you would not be able to lift him in your hands until he is alive.'

Meera went into extreme shock. The day she imagined to be lovely and memorable turned into a terrorful dream which she just wanted to forget. She remained silent for a while and then spoke up with a heavy voice 'Mom, will you approve two of my decisions?'

'Yes beta, speak up your wish.' Preeti said.

'Mom, I want to go in defense to protect my motherland. I can't see my son now. I am not courageous enough to lift the pain of losing him again. I can't........ '

'I can understand your pain. Calm down! I am with you in every decision of yours.

After a day, that tiny one-day-born boy died. After resisting herself; Meera went to attend her child's funeral. She saw her child for the first and last

time. She pretended to be strong in front of the other people but when she returned home, she cried aloud. She kept on crying for the whole day. Preeti was consoling her but not stopping her from crying. She lost her husband, son, and grandson but still she was trying to stay strong. At last, her painful silence broke down in tears.

'Mom, I am back. Hug me.' A note with this message came along with the heavy box after two years.

'Your daughter has lasted her life in a bomb blast. Jai hind!'

Heavy box

'Your Son has lasted his life for his love.' A man in a well-uniformed dress said to an old lady who seemed to be waiting for someone at the door. He kept a heavy box there in the hall and left with gratitude in their eyes.

That old lady was about to cry but her eyes were filled with pride and satisfaction. She didn't show anything; she went inside and called her daughter-in-law who was about 7-month pregnant. That young girl was so excited because just before two days, his husband had promised to come for her. He went on the mission and after that, they decided to celebrate their anniversary together. He told her that he was bringing a silver anklet for her as a gift. She was eagerly waiting for her husband in a light pink saree with small earrings that matches her color of eye shadow. Her open hair with bold kajal and silver-colored bangles were

waiting for the anklets to decorate her bare legs.

That old lady entered her room and by rubbing her hair softly she said 'My daughter, come with me.'

When Meera Singh saw tears in her mother-in-law's eyes, she asked 'Mom, why are there tears in your eyes?'

'No nothing. Just come with me.' That old lady said whose eyes were not accepting the pain of losing his young son.

Meera excitedly came outside in the hall to see his husband "Late. Tushar Singh". After coming outside, she saw that there was no one except the heavy box. She took the help of a chair to sit down and asked her mom-in-law 'Where is he? He lied to me; he sent gifts instead of coming. I will never talk to me. How could he...'

'Beta, He can't talk now.' Preeti Singh, her mom-in-law said in between her talks.

Meera lifted her face and asked curiously 'What happened? Why are you saying this? Is everything alright? What, speak up Mom?' she was sweating in tension.

'Calm down! My child, please. It is hard to accept but you have to accept the truth that your husband has sacrificed his life for this motherland...'

Without uttering any word, she started opening that box. The first thing, she saw after disclosing the box was the anklet that he promised to gift her. She took it out from that box and tied it in her bare feet. She stood up to go back to her room but

then; after moving four steps she felt dizzy and fainted.

Preeti alleged first but sprinted towards the hospital. Meera got admitted to I.C.U for immediate surgery as her condition was incompetent.

After performing surgery for two hours, finally, the doctor came and said 'I am sorry, your grandson has been born unhealthy. We have to keep him under 24-hour observation. Maybe he will not survive for long. We are trying our best to rescue his life but it seems to be impossible. Remain strong and support your daughter-in-law this time!'

'What?' Mrs.Preeti Singh said in a crying tone and sat on the chair nearby the ward. She was worried about the patient lying inside with closed eyes and disappointing silence on her face. Everything seemed to be blurry and disagreeable. She wanted to scream and cry aloud but she couldn't. It is impossible to measure the emptiness and sorrow inside her. 'What would happen when Meera will come to know about this? She would die after realizing the thing ambulating around.' All this thought was striking in her mind while sitting alone. Preeti moved inside the hospital room and sat beside Meera's bed.

She softly rubbed Meera's head and whispered 'Everything will be alright my daughter. I know that you are strong but you need to be stronger now.'

Meera suddenly started opening her eyes after

hearing the whisper of her Mom. She said in a strong voice and tears in her eyes ' Mom, Why it happened to me? I lost everything. Why? Am I so bad that everything got snatched from me? I know Tushar sacrificed his life for our safety, but how to accept this truth that he will never come again to meet me and our child.' She then asked about his son whose first cry disturbed her ears while being senseless.

'You have to be strong now. I don't want to say that but I have to say it; your child is unhealthy and he would not survive for more than a day or two. I am so sorry to say that but he is still under observation and you would not be able to lift him in your hands until he is alive.'

Meera went into extreme shock. The day she imagined to be lovely and memorable turned into a terrorful dream which she just wanted to forget. She remained silent for a while and then spoke up with a heavy voice 'Mom, will you approve two of my decisions?'

'Yes beta, speak up your wish.' Preeti said.

'Mom, I want to go in defense to protect my motherland. I can't see my son now. I am not courageous enough to lift the pain of losing him again. I can't........ '

'I can understand your pain. Calm down! I am with you in every decision of yours.

After a day, that tiny one-day-born boy died. After resisting herself; Meera went to attend her child's funeral. She saw her child for the first and last

time. She pretended to be strong in front of the other people but when she returned home, she cried aloud. She kept on crying for the whole day. Preeti was consoling her but not stopping her from crying. She lost her husband, son, and grandson but still she was trying to stay strong. At last, her painful silence broke down in tears.

'Mom, I am back. Hug me.' A note with this message came along with the heavy box after two years.

'Your daughter has lasted her life in a bomb blast. Jai hind!'

Heavy box

'Your Son has lasted his life for his love.' A man in a well-uniformed dress said to an old lady who seemed to be waiting for someone at the door. He kept a heavy box there in the hall and left with gratitude in their eyes.

That old lady was about to cry but her eyes were filled with pride and satisfaction. She didn't show anything; she went inside and called her daughter-in-law who was about 7-month pregnant. That young girl was so excited because just before two days, his husband had promised to come for her. He went on the mission and after that, they decided to celebrate their anniversary together. He told her that he was bringing a silver anklet for her as a gift. She was eagerly waiting for her husband in a light pink saree with small earrings that matches her color of eye shadow. Her open hair with bold kajal and silver-colored bangles were

waiting for the anklets to decorate her bare legs.

That old lady entered her room and by rubbing her hair softly she said 'My daughter, come with me.'

When Meera Singh saw tears in her mother-in-law's eyes, she asked 'Mom, why are there tears in your eyes?'

'No nothing. Just come with me.' That old lady said whose eyes were not accepting the pain of losing his young son.

Meera excitedly came outside in the hall to see his husband "Late. Tushar Singh". After coming outside, she saw that there was no one except the heavy box. She took the help of a chair to sit down and asked her mom-in-law 'Where is he? He lied to me; he sent gifts instead of coming. I will never talk to me. How could he...'

'Beta, He can't talk now.' Preeti Singh, her mom-in-law said in between her talks.

Meera lifted her face and asked curiously 'What happened? Why are you saying this? Is everything alright? What, speak up Mom?' she was sweating in tension.

'Calm down! My child, please. It is hard to accept but you have to accept the truth that your husband has sacrificed his life for this motherland...'

Without uttering any word, she started opening that box. The first thing, she saw after disclosing the box was the anklet that he promised to gift her. She took it out from that box and tied it in her bare feet. She stood up to go back to her room but

then; after moving four steps she felt dizzy and fainted.

Preeti alleged first but sprinted towards the hospital. Meera got admitted to I.C.U for immediate surgery as her condition was incompetent.

After performing surgery for two hours, finally, the doctor came and said 'I am sorry, your grandson has been born unhealthy. We have to keep him under 24-hour observation. Maybe he will not survive for long. We are trying our best to rescue his life but it seems to be impossible. Remain strong and support your daughter-in-law this time!'

'What?' Mrs.Preeti Singh said in a crying tone and sat on the chair nearby the ward. She was worried about the patient lying inside with closed eyes and disappointing silence on her face. Everything seemed to be blurry and disagreeable. She wanted to scream and cry aloud but she couldn't. It is impossible to measure the emptiness and sorrow inside her. 'What would happen when Meera will come to know about this? She would die after realizing the thing ambulating around.' All this thought was striking in her mind while sitting alone. Preeti moved inside the hospital room and sat beside Meera's bed.

She softly rubbed Meera's head and whispered 'Everything will be alright my daughter. I know that you are strong but you need to be stronger now.'

Meera suddenly started opening her eyes after

hearing the whisper of her Mom. She said in a strong voice and tears in her eyes ' Mom, Why it happened to me? I lost everything. Why? Am I so bad that everything got snatched from me? I know Tushar sacrificed his life for our safety, but how to accept this truth that he will never come again to meet me and our child.' She then asked about his son whose first cry disturbed her ears while being senseless.

'You have to be strong now. I don't want to say that but I have to say it; your child is unhealthy and he would not survive for more than a day or two. I am so sorry to say that but he is still under observation and you would not be able to lift him in your hands until he is alive.'

Meera went into extreme shock. The day she imagined to be lovely and memorable turned into a terrorful dream which she just wanted to forget. She remained silent for a while and then spoke up with a heavy voice 'Mom, will you approve two of my decisions?'

'Yes beta, speak up your wish.' Preeti said.

'Mom, I want to go in defense to protect my motherland. I can't see my son now. I am not courageous enough to lift the pain of losing him again. I can't........ '

'I can understand your pain. Calm down! I am with you in every decision of yours.

After a day, that tiny one-day-born boy died. After resisting herself; Meera went to attend her child's funeral. She saw her child for the first and last

time. She pretended to be strong in front of the other people but when she returned home, she cried aloud. She kept on crying for the whole day. Preeti was consoling her but not stopping her from crying. She lost her husband, son, and grandson but still she was trying to stay strong. At last, her painful silence broke down in tears.

'Mom, I am back. Hug me.' A note with this message came along with the heavy box after two years.

'Your daughter has lasted her life in a bomb blast. Jai hind!'

In the big house

By Nimi Kurian

"**S**mitha, please stop staring into the neighbour's house," said her mother, as she came into the apartment.

"I'm not staring ma, I'm looking…"

"Same difference, Smitha. This is a nosey behaviour you have developed recently."

The apartment Smitha lived in overlooked a large house with a garden. The owners had four cars parked in the front. They had also had two friendly Labradors. Every time Smitha passed the gate the dogs ran out to greet her. But the surly Gurkha would glare at her and send her on her way.

Recently, the son had married. Smitha watched all night as the fairy lights danced on the trees and bushes of the lawn. The sound of loud music and people talking and having a good time filled the silence of the night. Smitha saw the bride too – young, beautiful and full of life as she danced and laughed with her friends. The groom was handsome but sullen. Smitha wondered why. In her overactive nine-year-old head it seemed unusual to be unhappy when you were getting married.

In the first few days after the marriage, she saw the bride come out to greet visitors, see them off, or play with the dogs. Abruptly she stopped coming outside. Then one day, while the bride was walking on the terrace she had turned and saw Smitha at the balcony. The bride waved. Smitha waved back. After that, every evening the bride would come up on to the terrace and Smitha would stand on her balcony and they would talk.

Smitha learned that the bride's name was Meghna. She was from a small village far away. She said her parents were poor and so when these rich people came and asked for her hand her father was more than happy to agree. He didn't have to spend any money, said Meghna.

A month later, one evening Smitha noticed that Megha had a bruise on her face. When Smitha asked her, she said, 'O so careless of me. I walked into the door.'

They spoke for some more time and Smitha left her saying 'Watch where you are walking next time.'

Meghna did not appear on the terrace for the next couple of weeks. Smitha began to worry for her new friend.

"Ma, can I go over to that big house and see Meghna? I haven't seen her in a long time and I am worried…" said Smitha.

"Why should you be worried?" asked her mother.

Smitha shrugged.

One rainy evening, when Smitha looked out of her balcony she saw Meghna through the window of her house. She tried to call out but the noise of the rain drowned her voice. She waved, then she held her towel in her hand and waved, jumping up and down as she did so. Meghna must have noticed the motion from the corner of her eye because she turned around. Her face lit up like a thousand-watt bulb. She pointed her finger to the ceiling saying she would come up to the terrace.

When Smitha saw her, she was shocked. Gone was the beautiful, laughing bride. Instead, she saw a thin, stick-like figure, dressed in old faded clothes that were too small for her. Meghna said she was hungry. Smitha was shocked. She couldn't understand how someone could live in such a big house and still be hungry. She thought only poor people were hungry. They spoke for a while and when Meghna walked off, Smitha noticed that she was limping.

That night, when her mother got back from work she spoke about Meghna. Her mother said, maybe she had a fall, she explained about the limp. When she told her that Meghna was hungry her mother frowned but said, maybe she is on a diet. "You know all these young girls are always on one diet or the other."

That night, Smitha was startled awake. She

thought she heard a scream. But, she was not sure. She got out of her room and walked to her mother's room across the hall. She was surprised to see her mother standing on the balcony. Her mother did not hear her. Smitha walked to the balcony and saw one room on the ground floor was lit. A curtain had not been drawn. Meghna stood with her back to a cupboard. A man dressed in a white pyjama suit, his bald pate shining under the light of the tube was approaching her with a stick in hand. He was threatening her. Then with one hand he pulled her towards him and tore her clothes.

Smitha gasped. "Ma, isn't the Meghna's father-in-law?"

It was then that her mother noticed her. She pulled her inside. She was shivering. Smitha was puzzled. Why was that man beating Meghna? Where was Meghna's husband? Wasn't that Meghna's father in law? What was happening? Whatever it was, it wasn't anything good. She felt her mother's hand on her shoulder.

"I'm sorry Smitha. I should have listened to you earlier. You tried to tell me..."

"Tell you what ma?"

Her mother shook her head and got up. "It's not too late. We can still help."

Determinately she picked up her phone and made a few calls. Then she held Smitha's hands and said, "Come. We have work to do. You are never too young to learn."

Smitha and her mother changed out of their night-clothes and went downstairs and walked to the gate of the big house. The Gurkha glared at them. The two of them just stood there, silently. Smitha did not know what was happening. But since her mother had told her it was something that she had to 'learn' she too waited silently. Soon, a jeep drove up. It was a police jeep, with several policewomen. Behind them came a Maruti car with three women in it.

The policewoman who was sitting by the driver marched up to the Gurkha and asked him to open the gate. She was so commanding and forceful that he scurried to obey. The jeep drove in. The Maruti car went in behind the jeep. Smitha and her mother hurried in before they shut the gates. The police officer knocked on the door and rang the bell. They heard the dogs barking. Then raised voices. And above all that din the sound of Meghna's shrill screams.

The door flew open and the man in the white py-jama suit stood there. He was flustered, yet angry and indignant.

"What is the meaning of this?" he screamed.

"You tell us what is the meaning of this?" said the senior police officer, pointing her lathi behind him.

He turned to see and visibly paled when he saw the half-clothed figure of Meghna. Her face was bruised and tears coursed down her cheeks. Behind her stood the wife and son. The police office waved Meghna forward with her lathi. They wrote down everything Meghna said.

Smitha could not follow most of what Meghna said. But, she heard how she was often beaten, starved and punished for not doing what she was asked to do.

It was almost early morning when the women in the Maruthi car took Meghna away. The police took the other three. Smitha wanted her mother to take Meghna to their house. But her mother said, 'Maybe later. Now we have to observe pro to call.'

As they walked back to their apartment, her mother said, "Be strong always. Challenge any wrong you see. Stand up for what is right."

Identity

By Diya Desai

Nalini and Amit are happily married for 6 years but they weren't all flowery for them. After 2 miscarriages, emotional breakdowns and societal question marks, Nalini finally conceived normally in the third attempt. The news was surely a big thing for the couple.

Two more months passed. Nalini was in her second trimester and they even had a small party at their house announcing the beginning of parenthood.

A bright morning, Nalini was running late for office. She made her entry in register and inquired the receptionist, "Where is Mr. Das?"

"Boss is in a meeting with the Sen Industries," the receptionist replied.

"Okay.... Wait, Sen Industries? Our regular clients?"

"Yes ma'am."

"But I didn't receive e-mail for the meeting, wait,

let me check."

"Ma'am, you weren't sent the mail. Boss denied to do so,' the receptionist informed Nalini.

Nalini was really confused.

"Okay, when Mr. Das gets out, just inform him that I'm waiting for him in his cabin."

"Sure ma'am and ma'am, lifts aren't working still. You'll have to climb the stairs to the fourth floor.

Nalini headed towards the stairs and then waited for Mr. Das in the cabin. After about half an hour, Mr. Das enters his cabin.

"Oh, Nalini, how are you? Anything urgent?"

"I am fine, sir. Sir, why wasn't I sent an email for today's meeting? After all, they are my clients. I must have been present."

"About that, Nalini, I was going to inform you. Actually, you are shifted from that project."

"But why sir, did I make any mistake?"

"Not at all, Nalini. It's just that you're pregnant and after few months, you wouldn't be able to work on it anyway so I just did it now."

"But sir, I had already discussed with you that I'll complete most of the work before going on maternity leave and the rest would be completed by my team and I would personally supervise it. Then, why this?"

"Nalini, we really care for our employees. We don't want you to take stress in such crucial times."

"Sir, that's a nice gesture. But I am pregnant and not handicapped. Doctor has clearly mentioned that I could work till my due date and my job profile doesn't include running around the office. It's completely desk work."

"Oh, doctors just exaggerate everything. We know pregnant ladies get mood swings and eventually it will affect your efficiency. We can't compromise on our quality because of your pregnancy."

"Wow, sir. You know better than doctors. Then, you must also be knowing that lifts aren't working since a week and I'm going up and down four floors each day; you must be knowing that my desk is just 2 metres away from the pantry and the food smell is irritating for me and despite requesting to HR, my desk isn't changed. Sir, my sole point is that I will head this project as I'm catering the clients since 4 years. Right from product specifications to 3D model to prototype, I have been their product designer for many product launches. I want my clients back, that's it."

"That can't happen, Nalini. I've already appointed and introduced Arjun as the new head to the clients."

"Wait, Arjun? Do you mean, Arjun who is working for merely 2 years for this company? You know what, thank you sir for showing me my position. I wouldn't like to work further for this company. I am done."

"Nalini, you won't get such a job anywhere. You are just over-reacting the situation."

"No sir, you have underrated me. My resignation letter would reach you soon."

Nalini exits his cabin furiously.

At night, Amit returns from his office.

"Hey, Nalini. How was your day? You seem a bit off. Everything okay?"

"I quit my job."

"What? Why?"

"Mr. Das removed me from my project which I have been handling for years and replaced me with a junior. I still can't believe it."

"What but why did he do so?"

"Just because I am pregnant."

"Oh, then what's the problem, Nalini. It's good for you : less stress, more rest."

"Oh god, not again. Amit, I am pregnant. I am not suffering from some disease. Doctors clearly say that more activity would cause lesser complications during delivery. And my work is happiness for me, not stress."

"Ok fine, I don't want to stretch on this. Consider it as your leave. You can search for a job after your delivery."

"No, Amit. I don't want to do jobs. I want to open my own studio. I've been thinking about this for long."

"What? Is this some new mood swing of yours? Come on, Nalini, what's this childish thought?"

"What's so funny about this, Amit?" Nalini grew more serious.

"No, I mean industries prefer established companies for this and not any freelancers. See, Nalini, it's just the boiling anger inside you that's making you think of this business and all but once it cools down, you'll laugh on this. Business is no play and it needs money."

"I know what it takes to start a business and about money, I have some good amount of savings and for the rest of it, I can take a business loan."

"Okay, whatever, but I won't let you do this now. You have conceived with difficulty and I can't take the chance. We can think about this after our child is atleast 2 years old. No more discussion on this. I'm going to freshen up."

Weeks passed. Everything seemed well but Nalini was unable to distract herself. Her mind was sub-consciously busy planning for her studio but her conscious mind knew it isn't so easy - pregnancy, finance, studio space, projects, employees, etc. But one evening, Amit saw a new and super-excited avatar of Nalini.

"What happened? Why so happy? Share it with me too."

"Amit, Amit, I can't believe what happened today. This was so unexpected and uncalled."

"But atleast tell me what happened exactly?"

"You remember the project I was shifted from. Mr. Aditya Sen, the CEO of the Sen Industries came here and asked me to handle that same project. I am so excited."

"Wow, so you are re-joining the company, that's nice."

"No, not at all. He clearly said that they are very much happy with my work and hence, want me to complete this project. They broke the contract with the company. Amit, see now even projects are coming up, can't we think of the studio once again?"

"Not again, Nalini. They came to you because they knew that their tastes and preferences were catered by you since years and hence, their work would be easy. This is a project that you were already handling and it came back to you. Did you get any new projects?"

"How would I get? Did I advertise about my work or my studio? Just consider this as a good beginning."

"Nalini, I am tired of these monotonous discussions. You work at home, get done with this project and that's it."

The next morning, Nalini was busy watering the plants in her balcony. The door opened and Savita, her house help entered and seemed quite happy.

"Madam, have these sweets."

"Okay, but tell me the good news."

"Madam, I am starting my own buz...bijh..bijhnes."

"You mean, business?"

"Yes, yes, madam."

"Wow, great. But you were working in that restaurant, right?"

"Yes, madam. But they are very bad people. I wash so many dishes, sometimes till 12-12.30 at midnight but still they pay Ramesh more than me. I work so hard and get only half amount of it in return. So, I left that job, I also have some self-respect, madam."

"You are really brave, Savita. It is the same every-where. People consider women as weak and less capable."

"Madam, it is because they haven't felt the labour pain. If they would have, they wouldn't even think so."

"Yes. Anyway, but how will you manage? I mean you work all day and at night, business? But you didn't mention what business you are starting?"

"Madam, I have started 'Savita Pottery Store'. I used to make pots and clay utensils since I was a small girl and I like it. So I will manage. I will sell them in night markets and weekend trade mar-kets."

"God will help you and you will earn a lot of money."

"Thank you, madam. God bless you too."

"But, Savita, did your family agree? I mean busi-ness is a big decision."

"Madam, they are happy and anyways, whole day, I am a mother, a wife, a daughter-in-law and a house help so at the end, atleast I deserve to do some-thing I like."

"Yes, you are right. We women always find our identity in being someone's daughter, wife, mother, sister etc. but forget that we too are indi-viduals. Above all, firstly, I am Nalini and you are Savita."

"Yes, madam. Madam, you take rest. I complete my work."

Nalini nodded and went into deep thoughts. After

few minutes, she wrote a post on her social media account for vacancy for a product designer in Pune and left her contact number.

In the evening, her phone buzzed. She had received pictures of someone's resume. She was just checking it out when she got a call.

"Hello."

"Hello, am I speaking to Nalini ma'am?"

"Yes. May I know whom I am speaking to?"

"Ma'am, my name is Mitali. I just sent you my application for the vacancy of product designer."

"Oh okay, it seems good. Can you come tomorrow evening along with your portfolio at Blueberry Cafe? "

"Yes, sure ma'am."

The next evening, they met and Nalini took her interview.

"Mitali, you credentials are quite nice. The only thing I wanted to clarify is that I am a freelancer and for now, I just have 1 project in hand so salary would be 25% less than market rates. Do you still wish to apply for this? I mean you have a good portfolio, you can apply somewhere else too."

"Ma'am, salary isn't a concern. Product designing is my passion and the reason behind it is you. I have been following your work on social media and I'm a big admirer of it. So, working with you is a dream come true. Secondly, I went for a few job interviews but they are more interested in my marriage plans and my talent is a secondary thing for them."

"Oh god ! I don't understand when would these companies be a little more sensible towards young & talented girls, working women and new mothers. For such people and companies, female employees are more of a burden rather than assets. Don't worry. You are hired. I am looking forward to work with you."

It's been 3.5 years since that interview.

"Ma'am, the 'Vibrant Industries Summit' committee has shortlisted us for the event, the meeting is tomorrow and we have to complete the model in two weeks."

"Great news, Mitali. Just send an email thanking and assuring them that Nalini Design Studio would give its best."

"Sure, ma'am."

"And do one more thing, divide our staff into 4 teams of 4 each. Two teams would work on the Summit project while other two teams would work on our other 3 projects."

"Okay ma'am, I'll get it done."

Meanwhile, Nalini got a call.

"Hey Amit, did you pick up Sid from playschool?"

"Yes and he has a surprise for you. His teacher asked the name of his superhero and do you know what he replied?"

"What, Ironman?"

"No, he said 'Mumma'"

Nalini's eyes were filled with tears of happiness.

"Hey, you there?"

"Yes, yes."

"So Miss. Superhero, would you mind a dinner date with us boys?"
"I am open for it."

Sakhi

By Rashmi Navada

I always dreamt of my name being synonymous with quality reporting. Being a feature-writer for City Times, today would be the day that would take me a step closer to my dream. I have grabbed a spot for interviewing the elusive Ms. Neelanjana Mahesh. It would be her first interview ever- be it print, television, or the internet. They take her name in awe and respect in social services. She is the woman behind the NGO that sponsors mid-day meals in state-run schools. For countless women, her NGO is the temple, and she the goddess. But, there are only a handful of people who have seen her in person. I hope today I will be on that list of people.

A receptionist announces her presence. Wearing a full-sleeve, golden yellow tussar silk kurta with bright red palazzos and handmade sandals, Ms. Mahesh is almost 6 feet tall. A red dupatta covers her head and face. Side bangs escape the drape, covering her forehead. Dark glasses complete the chick-look. She sits on the chair with her back to the window; the sunlight giving a halo effect.

"You have pulled quite a few strings to interview me, Ms. Sen," she starts without preamble.

'Yes, mam. This is for a series I am writing called Spotlight. Every week we focus on a woman icon who has made a difference to society."

She gives a slight nod. I guess she is not one for small talks. I get straight to the point.

"We can start from your childhood and continue from there."

She takes some time before talking, as if she is filtering her thoughts. "I come from a lower-middle-class family. I lost my father when I was six years old. On compassionate grounds, my mother got appointment as an attender in the same bank my father was working. My father's family had disowned him when he married my mother against their wish. My mother was an orphan. So it was only my mother and me."

"Majority of the salary went into paying the rent and my school fees. My parents had always insisted on an excellent education as a measure of success. I was good at studies and I aimed to become a doctor when I grew up. I now hold a doctorate in Social Work instead." A hoarse laugh escapes her.

"Father's death caught us by surprise. There were no savings. We struggled to survive. Sanjeevini's parents paid my school fees."

She stopped the narration. It looked like she had gone into the past.

"Who is Sanjeevini?" I prompted her back to the present.

"My mother and Sanjeevini were the only constants during my growing-up years. Sanjeevini was my classmate from kindergarten."

"People around us often wondered how we, opposites could be friends. She came from a rich family of doctors. While she was short-tempered, I was the cool-cucumber. She took life easy while for me it was a serious affair. The only thing common between us was our dream of becoming doctors. What made our friendship strong was that we completed each other."

She had gone into that flashback mode again.

"So what led you to social work instead of medicine?"

She gave a slight shudder and continued with her story.

"Sanjeevini and I joined the same medical college. If not for that unfortunate incident, I would have been a doctor," she said.

"I was in my second year. One night while I was outside my house feeding the stray dogs. A man stopped near me asking for an address. As I got up to answer, he threw something at my face and rode away."

"The next thing I heard was a howl. To date, I don't know if it was me or the dogs. It was as if someone had poured boiling water. It felt like chili powder being rubbed on raw skin."

I sat transfixed. "What happened that night?"

"This happened that night." Slow paced, she removed her glasses and dupatta.

I got up with a hiss, pushing the chair. Both the chair and the recorder fell with a thud to the ground. The sound brought the receptionist hurrying through the door.

After confirming that her boss was doing ok, she placed the chair back at the exact spot as before and handed me the recorder.

Ms. Neelanjana dismissed the receptionist with thanks.

"Let me know when you are ready." She sits with her elbows on the arms of the chair with the fingertips drumming a noiseless tune.

I realized then why she never gave interviews. It was also clear why there were no photos of her anywhere.

The incident had marred the entire left side of her face, and the left eye was only a slit. Both her eyebrows were missing. Scar tissue in part covered her right eye. The side bangs covered the damage to the forehead, and the mouth was lopsided with the burnt skin stretched tight. The damage was visible on the neck too. She was the victim of an acid attack.

"Mam..." I am at a loss for words.

"I would like to call myself a survivor of acid attack and not a victim," she says as if reading my mind.

"I would have been a victim if I had killed myself. The close-range attack melted my ears and nose. It dissolved the skin on the cheekbone, forehead, chin, and neck. While I lost my left eye completely, my right eye is partially blind."

"The doctors decreed around 30 to 40 surgeries to just recreate the melted body parts. They were clear from the beginning that the surgeries would prevent infections. They would only bring back the functionality of the organs. These would cost me anywhere between 40 to 80 lacs. Cosmetic procedures would cost extra."

She went on with a flow. "Money was a huge issue. My mother sold some jewelry she had and the bank raised funds. Still, it was not enough."

"My mom put Ads in the newspapers asking for help."

"An NGO that provides medical help to the needy contacted us on seeing the Ad. They spoke to the doctors concerned and agreed to bear the remaining cost of the surgeries."

She looks vulnerable as she continues.

"The major intent of an acid attack is to deform and not to kill the person. The attacker condemns the person to lifelong suffering. I wished every day that he had killed me. The mirror became my worst enemy. I turned suicidal. It put my mother under undue stress. "

"I had no relatives. Curios neighbors saw me like a piece of the exhibit. Their comments and stares drove me insane. I had no one to talk to, not even

Sanjeevini. She had stopped talking to me for the last few months. I did not know why and now in this situation I was not interested in finding out."

"So did you find out who the man was?" I asked her.

"I hadn't made note of his vehicle number, nor I could see him because of the helmet. We filed a complaint, but with no leads, the police could not do much."

"Though it was a closed case for the men in uniform, for me it was still open. I went into depression. I quit college. With my eye not wholly working, it was not possible to pursue medicine."

"Amidst all this emotional and physical trauma, the NGO kept me alive and sane. They provided me, in-house counselors. Their work inspired me to the field of Social Work."

"My mother who had been my pillar passed away 3 years after my attack, leaving me all alone in the world."

Tears were streaming down her eyes as she relived those days.

"I helped in the day-to-day functioning of the NGO. They gave me a room to stay. I worked part-time at a petrol bunk to fund my studies. The only condition they put was that I had to cover my face all the time so as not to scare the customers away."

A wry smile lights up her face.

"So how did you start this NGO?"

"Fifteen years after the incident, a lawyer paid me a visit at the NGO. My friend Sanjeevini had willed me her entire property and savings. She had been the only child of her parents. After her parents' death, she had inherited their savings and property. She had succumbed to cancer six months back."

"This NGO-SAKHI-stands on one of the properties she bequeathed. Today is the twenty-fifth founding anniversary. SAKHI provides financial help to patients who cannot afford medical care, especially cancer patients and acid attack victims. We give vocational training to destitute women and help them become financially stable. The NGO also works with the state prison to upskill or re-skill women convicts to enable them to lead a fresh life once out of prison."

"Sanjeevini valued you in her life. But I am curious as to why she never visited you if she knew your whereabouts?" I asked.

"I wish I knew." The receptionist comes in to remind Ms Mahesh of an appointment.

I get up with a smile on my face. The interview had thrown light on the life of one of the most influential women in the country.

"Thanks for your time, Mam." I make my way to the door.

I stop mid-stride at her question. "Don't you want my photo for the article?"

She walks over to the light by the window, waiting for me. With the photo and the interview in my hand, I walk to my car with a spring in my steps.

∞ ∞ ∞

The interview had re-opened one memory Neelanjana had buried. A memory she would take to her grave.

Along with the will, the lawyer had given her a letter from Sanjeevini. The contents were still imprinted in her brain.

"Dear Neelu. Words cannot describe what you were to me. You were the sister I never had. Your intelligence and gentleness were what I valued most in you. While you were shy and abhorred attention, I was bold and craved for it.

For all the guys trying to catch my eye, I had eyes only for Sunil. Remember him? Our senior? He was the son of my father's friend. I had feelings for him for quite some time. When I gathered enough courage to profess my love to him, he was quick to dismiss it. He had feelings for someone else. I was not used to rejections. I cried for days; not because he did not 'love' me, but because he had rejected me. And one day I saw him talking to you, all gooey-eyed. I felt betrayed. I cut you out of my life. In a fit of anger and jealousy, I paid my driver to throw acid at you. I hoped with your disfigurement, Sunil would love me.

It was only months later that I got to know from Sunil that you had rejected his proposal since you knew I loved him. I cried my heart out. I wanted to come, hug you, ask for your forgiveness. But I could not face you. The guilt ate at me slowly. I became an alcoholic. It took multiple visits to the rehab center to get me back to normal. Five years back, my parents died in an accident. Soon after, I was diagnosed with stage IV leukemia.

If you are reading this, you know I am dead. The only thing I ask of you is your forgiveness. May God give you all the happiness you deserve."

Sanjeevini had been my one and only friend-SAKHI. Hope she is at peace now and feeling proud of her friend.

The Fervor

By Sakshvii

It was a Wednesday morning when everyone had been stamping the front yard of the court. There stood a lady holding her child in her left hand and gently massaging her womb with her right hand to comfort her another child. She was eagerly waiting for her lawyer. The lawyer hesitantly walked towards her and asked, "Shreesha, Are you sure that you want to file this case? They are in a very good position and they are capable of doing anything to save them. Think about your children at least."

"My husband was also in a very good position and now look. What was his end? I'm not going to give up on justice. And my children would want the same," she replied with a firm voice. She walked around the court and sat on a bench. She kept nurturing her womb and was immersed in her thoughts. While her elder child was wondering the things that are yet to happen.

In the mid-'90s, a sudden encounter was planned by the police department of Uttar Pradesh and 13 were shot dead including the DSP Mr. Malhotra: Shreesha's Husband. Mr. Malhotra begged his colleagues to spare his life as he had a family to be taken care of. Since he was an honest person who would definitely report the fake encounter that had happened. So he was also shot dead and an imprecise allegation was also made. On hearing all those, Shreesha's world had shattered and she desperately wanted to prove her husband's innocence and here they stand.

Her elder child, Prathiksha Malhotra, 7 years old, went near her mom and said, "Mamma, Why everyone is looking at us? Why are they saying papa's name? What is happening?"

Shreesha made her sit near her and said, "Your papa is no more and his name shouldn't be stained right? I'm fighting to remove the stain. And you do the same if I fail. Okay?"

Prathiksha nodded her head and hugged her mother. "Before my life had started, it came to a dead end. I wanted to restart it for you, your sibling, and your papa. And I will!" she pledged to herself and decided to fight strong.

She found a job for herself and educated her children. And her second child, Helena Malhotra was also taught the same. She tried in every possible way to find justice for her husband. This society will neither help any needy nor let them satisfy their own needs. It emerges with different types of criticisms and will impose the same on others.

The two girls hadn't spent a single day without being teased in their schools. "Hey, your father is the one who was encountered for supporting the criminals. Right?" Those words hit them hard. They were grown watching her mother crying all day and hearing all the cussing from society. While the other children at their age were going to park and playing, Prathiksha and Helena went to the court along with her mother.

One sudden day Prathiksha came to her mother and asked, "Ma, Why don't we get what we deserve? Will we get that, at least once in our lifetime?"

Her mother smiled at her and made her sit on her lap. "Kanna, all my life, I was thinking over the same question and I haven't found my answer. Now, you're asking the same. As of now, I can say that we should fight till the day we get it," Shreesha said looking at her husband's photo.

Years passed by and nothing changed including their zeal. Both the girls studied very hard and excelled in academics. They hadn't made time for friends. They would always sit with their mother and talked a lot. On such days, Helena asked, "Ma, why do the bad persons are always treated well and the good persons always suffer much?" That question hit the other two so hard. Prathiksha took Helena's hand into hers and said, "Hel, remember one thing. If a person does a bad thing, it will definitely hit him like a ball in a loop. Sooner or later it surely will happen."

Prathiksha was doing her psychology in Delhi and Helena stayed with her mother. Prathiksha was so determined like her mother in getting the justice that her father had deserved. She worked hard with all her heart. There exists one thing about life. When you think that it can't be bad as it is now, it will turn worse. After all, life is always a million-dollar question with an indefinite answer. Right?

The next worst thing that had happened was Shreesha being diagnosed with cancer. The entire family was shattered. There were lots of questions about what should be done next. "Ma, why are you worrying so much? Else are you thinking that if you had a son, he would have fought for papa's justice? Don't worry, Ma. You raised us with the same strength and willpower. You are our iron lady and we'll fulfill your wish. We'll study hard and clear the UPSC exam and we sit in a position. Then the world will listen to us. And soon papa will be free of his stain. This is our promise to you, Ma." Both promised their mother and to themselves. And none of them had dropped a single tear when Shreesha had passed away.

Days after their mother's death, both of them had shifted to Delhi and started their preparations. They found themselves a job and a hostel to stay at. "How're we gonna manage things, Sha?" Helena asked her sister. "We can, Hel. Think of mamma and papa. We have to do this for them", Prathiksha replied and made her sister lie on her lap. She tousled her hair and both of their eyes were at the picture of their parents. They had studied so hard and they handled their time efficiently. They had no holidays, festivals, cinemas, and whatnot. They were so dedicated and committed to what they were doing. Each supported the other and became the backbone of the other. While everyone was out there enjoying their lives, the sisters had a rough patch to clean.

"Sha! Have this tea," Helena handed over a cup of tea. Prathiksha smiled at her and started drinking it. In the meantime, Helena started asking her questions about what she had learned and helped her revise them. Prathiksha felt so proud of her sister and her vision. At one point, they had realized that they were as strong as their mother was. With managing their jobs and their life, months rolled on. Prathiksha had taken the exams and was waiting for the results. As expected she cleared the exam and secured 25th rank. After her training, she was appointed as an IAS officer. Meanwhile, Helena was studying hard to clear her exams. And in no time Helena had become an Assistant Commissioner.

One good day, both of them walked into the same court where they were once humiliated. When she entered, everyone saluted her and were left with no words to describe the raging fire they had. But for the girls, old incidents flashed in their minds since that was where her mother had spent her life fighting for justice.

And finally, after 31 years, it was proved that her father was innocent and the persons responsible for his death were punished. Both of them cried for the first time after her mother's death. Many reporters tried to speak with them. But they refused and ran out of the court with teary eyes.

It should have really taken tons of courage and perseverance to achieve what these girls did.

"Not everything is gonna be destined unless you make them. Nothing is gonna come to your lap unless you chase them."

Being a woman means a lot. There might be many struggles in their lives to achieve what they desire. But, there always lies a key to success despite those struggles. In fact, they will make you stronger. So, spread your wings as much as you can. Let the others decide, whether they are gonna be hit by your wings or enjoy the air it provides.

The Strangely Familiar Stranger

By Barkha Sharma

It was a pleasant summer morning. There was no school that day, so she was free to spend her morning the way she wanted. She decided to pass her time by sitting on her father's scooter, which was parked just outside her house and let her mind wander. Her father, on the other hand, was busy working. He was seeing patients in a small clinic just inside the gates of the house. She could hear everything her father and his patients were talking about. She could even see them if she craned her neck just a bit.

Almost a teenager, she was hitting puberty. Her breasts were taking shape and were slowly getting more and more noticeable. She didn't like them much because now she had to wear a bra. She hated bras. She was wearing her favourite sky blue top with a little silver butterfly printed on the left side and a matching brown checkered skirt.

As she sat thinking about random things, she saw a man on a bicycle riding along the street. Just when he was past her house, he stopped and back-tracked. He hoisted his bicycle onto the stand and came towards her. He put a hand on her knee and asked what her grandfather did for a living. That was an odd question as everybody knew her grandfather and father. Moreover, there were two boards on the wall behind her, which carried all the information about their respective jobs. However, she answered him anyway. "He's an advocate."

He put his other hand on her other knee. She was starting to dislike his hands. They made her feel uncomfortable, and she just wanted to push them away. But she was a shy girl and also didn't want to come across as rude. His hands started to move up and down her thighs now. They were beginning to scare her. He leaned towards her a bit and asked her if her grandfather worked from home. His hands continued to rub her thighs, making her heart thump loudly inside her chest.

"No", she said in a slightly trembling voice.

She glanced towards her father. He was still talking to his patients and preparing their medicines. He had not noticed that man. He did not know that a strange man was touching his daughter and scaring her. She looked back at the man. This time, she looked at his face instead of his hands, which were still on her thighs. He looked familiar. Had she met him before? Or perhaps he passed that street often? Or maybe he lived in the neighbourhood? Then, it hit her. He looked like the man who lived in the house across the park. That house and hers had a direct view of each other.

The man spoke again. Now, he asked her what her father did. She didn't understand why he was asking her such obvious questions. He could have just read the boards behind her or asked her father directly. He was standing right there in his clinic.

The man lifted his hand and moved it towards her chest. Just when one of his disgusting fingers brushed her breast, she pushed him away.

"I don't know!" she snapped at him and jumped down from the scooter.

She quickly walked inside her house. Her head was spinning, and her heart as ready to burst out of her chest. She hid behind the gates and peeked out to check if he was gone. Surely enough, he was riding away on his bicycle at a leisurely pace. He looked like he was secretly laughing at her. As if her fear was amusing to him. She felt a shiver go through her body. She looked down at her hands. They were shaking badly. In a matter of mere minutes, that man had managed to fill her with fear that chilled her to the core. The five awful minutes with him felt like hours that would not come to an end. All the while, she had been wishing and hoping that her father would look in her direction, or that her mother would look down from the balcony above, or someone would come out of the house and chase the man away. But no one came. She had to do it herself.

She did not know why she didn't call out to her father. Perhaps she thought he wasn't doing anything wrong and that it was she who was mistaken.

As she went inside, to the safety of her house, she kept thinking who that man was and where she had seen him. She did not want him to turn out to be her neighbour because that would mean that he could see her and come near her anytime. As the days passed, she kept an eye out for the neighbour, who looked like the scary man, but he never even attempted to come near her. So, she, hesitatingly, came to the conclusion that that man did not live around her.

She did not tell anybody about that incident – not even her parents or her friends. She did not forget about it either. She could not. She tucked the memory away in a dark corner of her mind, from where it would stare at her silently and sometimes demand her attention like a ghost.

Years later, she saw him again. Or she thought it was him for a second. It was actually her neighbour. His daughter was a student of hers. He had come to the school for a Parents- Teacher Meeting. That brief meeting left her feeling anxious. She plastered a slime on her face and talked to him and his wife about their daughter's education. But throughout that conversation, she could not help wondering if he was mistaken and he was really

that man.
And if he was, did he recognise her? Had he been watching her?
She was stronger now, more confident. She was a grown woman. But the little girl inside her could not get over that incident.

A girl who made it

By Vini Kunhappan

Born to a upper middle class family. Suhana had everything at her disposal. A good house, good education, her parents were financially well off. She on the other hand never really got to enjoy these privilages. First things first she was a girl, physically huge or in common words fat, born to a family who filled up their forms as SC(schedule caste) and to top it all highly opiniated,smart, intelligent who had a mind of her own. Which is a dangerous thing specially if you live in a country where Goddesses are prayed in temples only to be abused at home. We all know that "charity begins at home" but for Suhana it was "discrimination began at home".

Being the first child she was expected to look after her younger brother and cook for the family at a very young age,since she was in grade 5th. Where girls her age used to play after school. She use to prepare dinner, clean the house wash the utensils and look after her younger brother after school work . All this because both her parents were carreer oriented and were busy building up their lives. While Suhana on the other hand became far more mature than her age.

Her parents though highly educated never thought highly of Suhana but showered all their love on their youger son "the heir to their throne" Their only hope in their old age, because it is our culture where we think its the son who will take care of us when we are old and girls house is where her husband is". Her parents always cursed and taunted her for being on the heavier side. All her life her parents or her extended family always looked down upon her just to humilate her for her body. School and college for her was no different either. Her teachers thought she was dumb because of her physical appearence. But Suhana was not dumb she was bright at academics and good at science. Science fascinated her. She always stood first in her science projects. Still her achievements were always over shadowed by the narrow minded views of the society.

After graduation her parents hurried to get her married ,as girls of her age where already bearing babies. Suitable prospects showed up at her door only to rejecte her because here in our country even if the guy does not even have an ounce of personality its fine,but the girl should be ascended from the heavens. Typical patriarchy, I say. After multiple failed attempts and extensive promotional diets which her parents forced her into nothing worked as it turned out to be a hormonal issue. A body which which she has to live with for the rest of her life. Her family cursed her ,abused her, blamed their fate. Driving Suhana to a point to take her life. Guess God was on her side she survived the attempt, but scared for life. She knew she had to do something to get away from this. Her solution was to get herself admitted in one of the best law colleges. At first her parents were against it but they some how had to give in . That was a small victory for Suhana,a small step towards her freedom. They agreed only on one condition that they would help her get admitted but from there on she has to fend for herself. No extra money will be spared. She happily agreed. Once the admissions were finalised she immediately moved out into P.G accomadation

Here life was different she lived with other two students of her same age. These people made her realize what it meant to be living life on her own terms. Her first transformation came with her clothes from typical salwar kurta to jeans top . She was never allowed to wear one on the behest of what will people say. Her room mates loved her after all suhana was an extremely talented cook, who dished out cusines in a giffy. Her friends helped her to enjoy late nights which was ofcourse prohibited at her house. She sometimes envied these girls. She use to feel neglected by her family on seeing how her roomates were pampered and taken care off my their respective parents. On the other hand Suhana had to work partime to pull through college. Although her parents did quite well didn't think it was necessary to provide her. Once she had fallen extremely sick and ran out of cash. She called her parents for help. But her parents brushed it off saying that she is just making up her sickness and she just needs money. She cried all night thinking how her own parents could do that to her, which only led to detoriation of her health. Her friends did help her out that day but she swore not to ever depend on her parents for anything.

College was a place where she found solace. This place wasn't off limits for discrimination though.She was abused and harassed by her classmates for being from SC community. Some envied her because she had certain outlets at her disposal due to her religion or caste. She did feell bad about all these things,but her determination was too strong for her to be deterred by such lowly thinking people. Her love life was not easy either. She was approached by the opposite gender for her voluptuous appearence. She always joked about having big breast. She use to say that at any place her boobs arrived first and then herself. Every time she was touched by a man she was reminded of the time how her uncle tried to physically abuse her. That was a nightmare for her as she was asked to keep quite about the whole incident. So as to maintain the family name.

Over the years Suhana actually was getting comfortable in her skin after all these years of humiliation. Her grades were top notch and she made it through law college with flying colors. She was a gold medalist of her batch. Her vocabulary improved to a great deal. Something not expected to happen to children studying in vernacular medium school. On her happiest days also Suhana was reminded to come back home, so that her parents can scout for a groom. Now Suhana, advocate Suhana was firm on her decision. She immediately joined the law firm where she had interned and to her luck also won the first case of domestic violence for a woman client. Years went by Suhana now judge Suhana was a reputated personality. It took her parents so many years to come around her name and fame . They were proud of her and also a bit ashamed of their unwanted behaviour towards her.

Suhana took an early retirement to fullfill her family duties. She us married to a wonderful human being who not only understands her but also loves her unconditionally. She is blesseed with two beautiful children. Now managing her own law firm and helping out women in despair,she is also a beacon of girl education in her city. Suhana has come a long way from the discrimination, humiliation, underestimation and all the people who thought she couldn't make it - she definitely made it!

An Unmatched Victory

By Dikshita Bharadwaz

In the city of Meerut, lived a young girl named Shruti or, as others liked to call her, Shru. She belonged to a financially stable family and was the only child of her parents. Her father had a good business in textiles while her mother was a housewife. She was given every opportunity to educate herself and be responsible for her own fate. Thus, she had a pretty normal and calm childhood where there was no toxicity and madness. She was well protected by her parents and kept away from the harsh realities of life. But nobody realised that a storm was coming her way. A storm which would rip apart her happy and calm life and replace it with all kinds of miseries and chaos that she never expected,or even imagined.

The storm hit her at the age of sixteen, when she lost her father to cancer. Lung cancer. All the money that they had saved, property and business was lost in the failed attempt of saving him.

And thus when he left for his heavenly abode,they had nothing to survive on. No food,no home. They would've been on the streets if Shru's uncle didn't come to their rescue.

So, just like a light source on the darkest of nights, her Rahul Chacha entered their life as a ray of hope. He took them with him to Lucknow, her father's birthplace. Rahul Chacha lived in their ancestral home with his wife and two sons. The elder son was nineteen and the younger one was thirteen. She resumed her studies there and started to live a normal life. But not until long. Her aunt,who was pretty supportive when they first arrived, now started anticipating their departure. She would hear her fighting with her uncle every other night over this issue. And her uncle would everytime turn down her demands of sending Shru and her mother away. It was as if he had some kind of benefit from their stay at his place. What benefit?

Well, that will be revealed in the right time and the right place. Months passed and everything was smooth and calm like usual. But one day, something happened. Something that changed everything. Something that no one expected. It was a spring afternoon and Shru was in her room taking a nap. Her mother was in a nearby temple with her aunt and both her brothers were in tuition. She was alone in the house with her uncle who had returned from his office moments before everyone left. She was sound asleep when someone grabbed her by her waist. She jumped up only to find that it was her uncle. He was on top of her and was indicating her to keep quiet. He then pulled off her clothes and raped her. Twice in a row. She sobbed and sobbed but couldn't scream. It was not like he covered her mouth. But more like her entire body was numb and had no energy to produce that scream. Her mind was dumbstruck and thus couldn't think of any way of getting out of that situation. It was as if her soul was ripped apart and her heart was shattered into a million pieces.

After he had done what he wanted to for a long time, he threatened her of throwing them out of his house if she uttered a word. She was afraid of him. Knowingly or unknowingly, they had given the control of their life to him. And now, he was using that same control to hide this sin that he had committed. And for the next three years, this happened almost every time they were home alone. She tried her level best to avoid being alone with him but somehow ended up in that situation. It was as if the fate was always in his favour. Her mother had no idea about all this. She was glad and thankful to her uncle for allowing them into her house and aiding her daughter's studies. Shru sometimes had an overwhelming urge to tell her mother about all this but then stopped thinking about the life on streets. And finally, she turned 19. It was big day for her because now she could move out of the house.

So after her little birthday celebration she made her entire family gather in the living room and put forward her wish of moving out. She believed that if not others,then at least her mother would agree to this. But unlike to what she thought,everyone,including her mother,refused to let her go. She didn't understand why. Maybe if her mother knew what was happening to her daughter then she would have let her go whole heartedly. But right now, she couldn't resist seeing her 'little daughter' leave her. But Shru was sure to lose her sanity if he lived there any longer. Being in a situation where your body is being used for sexual pleasures without your consent and there is absolutely nothing you can do about it, was mentally frustrating.

And Shru had been in this situation for three years now. And, honestly,at this point she was just exhausted of being in this situation and wanted to move out. But it seemed impossible to convince them. And so she made a plan. A plan of running away. It took her three days to put everything in place. She gathered all the supplies,which included some money, clothes, packets of chips and so on. And on the night of execution, she went to her mother's room and talked to her for about an hour. She knew she was going to hurt her mother. But this seemed the only way out of a life which was a living hell. And after everyone went to sleep, she sneaked out of the house and took a train from the nearest station to Meerut. Yes, Meerut.

The place where she was born. The place where her father died. The thought of being in the same streets where she once walked with her father was tormenting. But she was brave. Wasn't she? So,upon reaching Meerut she started looking for a job as well as a place to stay. And both were pretty difficult tasks. She even had to stay in a motel for two nights before she could find an apartment. Thanks to the money she brought. On the third day, she finally found an apartment.It was not very luxurious and had only one bedroom. And on top of that, she had to share with two other girls. She had never lived in a situation like that before but now she had learnt to adjust with every situation life throws in. She is no longer the same Shruti she was when she left. Rachel and Simran were her new roommates.

Both of them were very kind to allow her in the apartment but upon arrival she was given a list of do's and don't. For example, she was not allowed to bring any of her relatives in the house. Little did they know, that she was herself trying to run away from own relatives. Well, apart from letting her in Rachel did another favour to her. She gave her Richa's number. Richa Chadda, the owner of "Wonder Weddings" , a leading event management company and Rachel's childhood best friend. Shruti never thought of being an event planner but she couldn't deny a job opportunity. And so the very next day, she went to meet Miss Richa Chadda in her office. Upon entering, she was greeted wonderfully by two of her employees and was asked to sit. The place was very well decorated with images of all the weddings they had planned. When the employees realised that Shru wanted a job in the firm, they immediately contacted their boss and led her to her office upstairs.

It was a two storey building with different rooms assigned to different departments. Departments like the catering arrangement,the decorators, technical heads etc. And on the top floor was Miss Chadda's room. Shru thought that this lady would be very arrogant and self-centred but when she met her, she was dumbstruck with her down-to-earth behaviour. Richa was so kind and responsive that it shocked Shru to her core. Upon listening to what Shru had to say, Miss Chadda gave a job to her without hesitation and even agreed to teach her everything on her own.

Her first wedding as a wedding planner was a huge success and everyone in the firm liked her ideas and designs. She was shining the brightest amongst all. She continued to work with them in every event that came their way. And after nine months of being this wonderful employee, she received another shock.Shocks had become a daily part of her life. But for the first time in years, it was a good shock. Because, Miss Chadda, her boss, had presented her some papers. Papers which said that Miss Chadda wanted Shruti to become a partner in the company. Yes, you heard it right. A partner. This meant that she no longer was a mere employee but a boss herself. Which in turn meant that now she had a secure job. So she decided to finally go back to Lucknow and bring her mother with her. And also do something she had wanted to do for years. Finally,after so many years she was at a point where she no longer had to depend on her uncle for anything. And hence she thought of finishing the unfinished business. She travelled back to Lucknow and was met with all kinds of allegations from her family. She was given the tags of irresponsible,careless,rude etc. But then all of them became quite when she confronted her Rahul Chacha and asked him why he did what he did. He didn't utter a single word.

Of course, he knew he was guilty and had some-what realised that this girl had achieved some-thing to be able to look him in the eye and confront. Her mother was heartbroken for not being able to help her in her darkest phase but Shru managed to console her. And then they left for Meerut with a threatening that if he tries to find them then she would file a police complaint against him.Upon reaching Meerut, she immedi-ately shifted to a new apartment, that she had already finalized before going to Lucknow,and started living with her mother. Now this should have been the happy ending, right? But it wasn't. Not for her. She wouldn't call it a 'happily ever after' when she knew that someone somewhere is going through the same things she did and is not able to speak up. She wanted to be there for them. To be their strength. To educate them and make them capable of standing up for themselves. And that's what she did. She started speaking publicly about her experience and how she overcame it. She wanted to inspire all the girls to become capable enough to fight against such odds. And she continues to strive for that, even today.

By Dhatrika Thanughna

Sita, as the name suggests was a very talented girl. In her school she stood first in every field. Whether it be education, sports, creativity or anything the first place was always reserved for Sita. Her room was always filled with books, medals and certificates. She was indeed a blessing for her family. But was treated as an unwanted piece. Her grandmother always thought a girl child being born was awful. The doctor said Sita's mother could give birth only ones, if they tried for second pregnancy both the child and the mother would die. This was the only reason why Sita did not undergo feticide and die.

Sita's father's only duty was to get her married to a wealthy gentleman. Sita was married at a very early age when she was 16 to Mr. Vivek Verma.

Vivek, as the name suggests was a very intelligent

and wealthy gentleman. A match for Sita who won the hearts of her family just with his property. He was a very modern cultured man who thinks wives are "Glorified Servants".

Sita's in-laws always expected a baby boy, but in the sonography tests her womb had a baby girl. As soon as her in-laws come to know about the female fetus they decide to attempt feticide without Sita's knowledge and tell her that she has undergone miscarriage. Sita was never informed because she had the willpower to raise voice against her in-laws and if she comes to know that her fetus was killed she would take legal action on them. It was very simple, after the test if the doctors says, "Jai Shri Krishn" then it was male and if the doctor says, "Jai Mata Di" it was a female child. Knowing this is illegal and a crime the doctors just demanded bribes to do it. And Sita never knew why she underwent miscarriages for the first three times though she took a lot of care.

This time was Sita's fourth pregnancy when she was praying for a baby and not a miscarriage again and her in-laws wanted to know the gender of the baby at the hospital. After the sonography when the doctor came out, she announced that Sita and the baby were healthy. But this was not what her in-laws wanted to hear so they asked, "Doctor, the baby is a boy right?" and the doctor replied, "Sorry, I can't tell you the gender of the baby". For a time there went an argument about the baby's gender but fortunately the doctor won the argument and after a few months a cute, pretty little female infant was born. She was named Ria and after two years Sita gave birth to a male child Rahul.

Ria was always discriminated at house and Rahul though not doing anything was always appreciated. Because of this baised surroundings Ria in her tenth-standard was so much disturbed that she aimed to become a boy in future. Coming to know the changes in Ria's behavior Sita called her psychologist friend, Prachi and fixed an appointment with her where she decided to send Ria to live with Prachi for further studies because this surrounding would ruin her daughter's life as hers and also where Prachi and Mahesh have no children Ria would give them a better company.

Mahesh and Prachi took Ria's responsibility and cared her like their own daughter. Ria was then joined into a very good college. Ria was a skinny and fair girl who had a proper height but not weight. Being skinny she didn't had a proper figure which society would like her to maintain. Her class boys teased her 'punctured-tyre' based on the size of her breasts. Being teased 'skeleton' was quite normal for Ria but she couldn't take the word 'punctured-tyre'. She was an introvert and didn't share this abuse with anyone. She decided not to take them serious but was unsuccessful. Unknowingly she started feeling jealous of girls with proper figure and especially their breasticles. Days went on and nothing changed, one fine day she met Kunal, her senior and a very smart looking handsome person, in a debate. She loved the way he opposed physical abuse and went on to have friendship with him. They were very good and close friends and a few days later they decided to turn their friendship into a relationship. This was very much new and exciting for Ria. She was very new to love and relationships, she was in her own dream world with Kunal. Kunal was 20 and Ria was 18. She believed love has no age differences it just needs thought similarities and a heart connection.

Days later, Kunal called Ria on their first relationship anniversary to Raj Tilak Hotel. Ria told Sita and Prachi that she was going to celebrate her friend's birthday. Both Sita and Prachi wanted to give Ria her whole freedom; they didn't want to restrict her for anything and so sent her for the birthday celebration.

For their very first anniversary Kunal ordered a Red-Velvet cake and both of them holding hand in hand cut it. They had their dinner there in the hotel restaurant and then Kunal had a surprise for her. He booked a room in the hotel and asked Ria to close her eyes and enter the room. Ria was a bit scared and in a confusion of what to do but when Kunal pleased her she got convinced and joined him. The room was decorated with red and white balloons on the walls and floor, there were 3-4 pleasant scented candles lightening and a heart shaped with rose petals on the bed. It was like a paradise for her, she never experienced this. Being away from her parents in teenage and settling with another couple who were not her own parents and were both working, she never felt so much loved as she felt with Kunal and did as directed by him. Kunal made her feel special and asked her to get physical with him. For the advanced thinking and matured mindset loosing virginity at 18 was common but for Ria it was not and so she refused and ran away back home. She didn't inform anyone about what happened with her but just quietly cried whole night and woke up the next day with a smile hiding her sorrow behind it.

Kunal couldn't accept Ria leaving him with a breakup so he turned violent. He started blackmailing her that he would tell about their relation to her parents and announce it on social media. He started calling her with different numbers and offending her. She was being emotionally abused and started facing a mental-disturbance. This was the second time when Ria faced a mental disturbance. It was difficult for her to overcome it and she fell into depression. When Prachi noticed Ria behaving strange, she counseled her for a moment and came to know everything which happened with Ria. Prachi informed all this to Sita and they filed a case against Kunal and within a few days he was behind bars.

Sita wanted to take her daughter back to her house but couldn't because of her family which imposed domestic violence on her. Every night her husband would come home drunk. When she went with a food plate to feed him, he would throw the plate and beat her with his belt, and sometimes also throw the broken glass-plate pieces on her which pricked her. During the day her in-laws made jeers on her

and her son just did nothing but supported them. None of them treated Sita like a human and if she did raise voice against them, they threatened to harm Ria. The only reason behind Sita's survival was her daughter.

Sita advised Prachi to go some other far off city along with Ria and her husband where there would be no disturbance or distractions to Ria. Within a week, three of them shifted to a far of city and were in touch with Sita through texts and phone calls. Ria was preparing for her IPS examination with no disturbance. With whole hard work she passed the examination with AIR 1, went on for her training and finally achieved her dream of becoming an IPS Officer equal to a male.

Today was the day when she was being honored. After receiving the honor when she was asked to give a speech she said, "Good morning everyone, thank you for this honor. Becoming an IPS Officer might be a dream for at least one person sitting here but it was not mine. I never wanted to become an IPS Officer unless few incidents took place in my life. I don't actually have a very big success story but few reasons for choosing the Police Service field.

The first reason is my mom, Sita Verma. She was a topper and always first in every field at her school. But she was discriminated on the basis of gender by her parents and grandparents. And couldn't continue her studies further. When I was born, even I faced the same situation. I wasn't a topper but was good at studies but still was always depreciated and my brother though doing nothing was loved and cared. As a result of this discrimination at house I wanted to become a male in future because everything a male does either it be good or bad was accepted but if a female does something good she has to listen to jeers rest of her life. Then in my college days I underwent physical abuse and mental abuse. Here when I fell into depression my mom was suffering domestic violence, still she managed and gave me more importance and both my mom and my masi, Prachi stood for me, fought for me and gave me my whole freedom.

A woman is a person who plays multiple roles in her life for you. She becomes your daughter to make you proud, becomes your sister to support you, becomes your life partner to teach you the actual meaning of love, and becomes your mother to bring you up. Despite all these she works as a servant in the house but never calls herself a maid. She happily does all the household works. A woman who bleeds for seven days every month and doesn't die, who joyously spend her whole life for you, who gives birth to a new world inside her womb, who brings you in the world is considered weak and is abused, offended and insulted in our society. A female whose birth is awful but is expected to give birth after a certain age is suffering domestic violence. Why?

To answer these questions I decided to enter this field and whenever I catch a criminal who has committed these I will make sure to ask him the answer to my questions. But I join my hands and request you to respect womanhood because of which you are here listening to me. Today it is only because of my mom and my masi that I'm here standing in front of you all and receiving this honor. I thereby give my mom and my masi the whole credit of this honor." Listening to this tears rolled over the cheeks of Mr.Vivek Verma who was one of the audience there witnessing Ria's honor and in his mind with whole heart he thanked the doctor who didn't reveal the gender of Ria because of whom she is alive today.

Womanhood is not just about the state of being woman. It's about sacrificing for good like a woman. Womanhood is all about taking a step for change.

About The Authors

Aditi Jain, a resident of Bilaspur, Chhatisgarh, India, is currently doing her Masters in Medical Biotechnology. Her dream is to work as a scientist but also write a lot of fiction. She wants to create a fantasy fiction series for teenage and young adult women with strong ideals of inner strength and equality regardless of gender, socio-economic status, nationality, colour, and sexuality.

A foodie at heart and a music and literature lover, her favourite book of all times is "Pride and Prejudice" by Jane Austen.

She finds the FemmeFluenza event conducted by writerfluence, a commendable step towards gender equality and appreciates their effort to make the society a better place. Their efforts to support New Authors and provide them exposure is incredible.

∞∞∞

Afreen Shanavas is the co-author of multiple anthologies including A Mélange of Memories, Thrive, The Unheard Voices and Hope. Her work has also appeared in the Inframe magazine under The Great Indian Art Project.

She was born in India and moved to UAE where she spent most of her childhood reading fiction and watching Hollywood movies. Inspired by the storytelling of phenoms like Steven Spielberg and JK Rowling, she was drawn to the art of writing at the age of twelve.

When she isn't reading or writing, you can find her cycling, playing badminton or scrolling through Instagram.

Afreen now makes her home in God's own country with her family.

Alipi Das is a voracious reader and a passionate writer. Her inclination is towards classics from the Victorian era of Charles Dickens and the Bronte sisters, though she reads books of all genres. She is an active member of various writing clubs and enjoys her passion. Her works have been selected in some of the online competitions and published on their websites and magazines. Her short stories have been featured in anthologies and published in Amazon Kindle and paperback. She also loves painting and travelling. Cooking, listening to music and dancing are her stress busters. She is also an avid film aficionado. Humour and positive thinking are the mantras of her life.

Nineteen years old, AnweshaPanda is quite the girl next door, an introverted undergraduate student, a budding wordsmith and a voracious reader. Dan Brown's 'Angels and Demons' made her fall for reading. She inherited the passion for reading and writing from her father; and dancing from her mother. She loves to capture the world in a frame and grooving to zesty beats, finds bliss in sketching and painting. An animal lover and a strong karma believer who prioritises her family, friends and ambition the most. Still waiting for her letter from Hogwats. The world of literature and art has helped her discover a new self. Who knew the scribbler of last page of the notebook would be a writer someday. She has lately co-authored an anthology which would be out soon.

Barkha Sharma was born to middle-class parents. Her father was a Homeopathy doctor, and her mother, a homemaker. Although a reader since a young age, she was especially obsessed with novels during the last two years of her high school. She would borrow two or three books from her school library at a time for a week. Then read them under the pretence of doing her homework (of course, her parents knew that).

She went on to pursue a Bachelor of Arts degree in English Honors from the University of Delhi, so she wouldn't have to read novels in secret. She landed a job as a Content Writer even before completing her graduation. She did her masters in English literature on the side from IGNOU.

Currently, Barkha is a part-time writer while working full-time to become an editor. She aspires to become a full-time published writer and part-time traveller. Writing for FemmeFluenza,

Barkha says was intriguing. "It gave me an opportunity to get published. I did not expect to win, but when I did, I was over the moon. Moreover, I loved writing on the topic - women's survival in a phallus-centred society."

D. Thanughna is a teenager from Hyderabad, India who started her literature journey at the age 12. She is as keen as mustard in reading books and a passionate writer. It was not known to the world until the 2020 lockdown that she was quite good at writing. In the busy routine she couldn't make up time to pen her thoughts and feelings but lockdown came as boon for her when she took up writing jingles, quotes, stories and poetries again. She also made her first attempt in co-authoring an anthology which will be out soon.

Apart from writing Thanughna is in love with movies, songs and her rest place. She is a foodie and an energetic chocholate lover.

LoroseLorose

Dikshita Bharadwaz is sixteen years old and is

known for her ability to put every situation into words. She is someone who is very philosophical and likes to motivate others. She is passionate about writing and loves to pen down her thoughts whenever she can. She is very fun-loving and cheerful. She is determined about her work and does everything she can to complete her task on time. Hardwork doesn't bother her in any way and she doesn't give up on things easily. She is a great friend and likes to keep her circle tight .She is a good secret-keeper and is extremely reliable. She is a natural leader and is known among her peers for her leadership skills. She is ambitious and self-motivated. She has an extraordinary love for helping people in need and tries to do so as and when possible. She is a travel freak and has an exceptional longing for late night drives.

Diya Desai, was born in the city of diamonds, Surat in Gujarat. Though born in Surat, she spent her entire childhood in Valsad, a small and lush green town in the western most part of Gujarat. She is about to complete her schooling from St. Joseph E.T. High School, Valsad. Diya has been academically great throughout her entire school life. She also participated in various events like Olympiads, quiz, elocution, debate, poetry writing, essay and letter writing etc.

After her schooling, she wishes to pursue her career in Economics along with pursuing writing as her hobby and maybe later as a side profession. She loves being in the lap of nature, listening and humming to melodious music. You can either find her with books and her cycle or with her family. Me-time is her favourite pass time thing. Moon and music are food for her soul. She likes every medium which provides her space and freedom to express herself. So, she has a very special corner for language and arts. She enjoys being knowledge-able. Books are her best friends and pen-paper are her go-to people. Exploring people and places amaze her. Capturing and living the little moments of life is what she believes life is about.

Despite being only 17 years old, she understands the subtlety of human relationships. She has always been a voice for gender equality and supporting strong women. Women empowerment isn't a term she believes in because she strongly believes that every women has infinite strength, the task is to make them realize it.

Diya is a person ever-ready and ever-striving for serving humanity and art. She is young, determined and ready to set her good mark in the minds and hearts of readers.

Gowri Bhargav is a certified storyteller from Kathalaya academy. An Engineering graduate who is highly interested in arts, she has always had a passion to tell stories. Several storytelling workshops are being conducted by her for the benefit of school children.

She has also been rendering her stories online through several platforms. "Gowri Storyteller" is her youtube channel dedicated to storytelling for various age groups.

She has been an active contributor for "Talking Stories Radio" - a programme dedicated to the art of storytelling by East London radio. "BTB storyteller of the year 2020" was recently awarded to her by the jury panel of "Beyond the Box" - a Facebook group.

Gowri is a voracious reader and also loves to weave words into poems, short stories and micro-tales. She has won several online contests conducted by literary groups like Penmancy, Artoonsinn, Asian Literary Society, Pink Comrade, Poetry Planet and Writefluence. Her works have been published in various online portals, literary magazines, journals and anthologies.

Ishani Majmundar is a software engineer by profession and writer by passion. She is mother of a baby boy and her life revolves around her toddler. She is a true Libran who loves peace and harmony in Iife. She is avid reader and loves to write blogs, stories, short stories and poems. Apart from this, she loves art and craft, cooking innovative recipes and music. She writes with the intention of inspiring souls and touching hearts.

Manher Kaur, a girl of sixteen, started writing at a young age. She has spent a colossal time reading books throughout her entire school life. She has taken full advantage of the lockdown by developing a passion for fiction writing.

Although story writing was just a hobby in the beginning, the urge to write gradually grew stronger. With the aid of virtual courses on Literature writing, Manher Kaur gained the skills to conceptualize ideas and thoughts in her mind and put them on paper.

Her favorite themes include- suspense, mystery, thrillers, plot twists and she looks up to the works of Ernest Miller Hemingway and Agatha Christie as her inspiration.

Like a quintessential high school senior, she is not distinct about the path ahead. However, this new-found talent of writing will never wither away.

Minakshi was born in Bihar, India to a traditional family. Her father was a successful business man and her mother served in home as a housewife. She spent most of time with her mother who had a stock of stories inside her.

From primary school to high school, she grew up hearing lot of stories which had different genre and specifications. To complete her college studies, she headed towards Lovely Professional University, India.

She had started writing since she was in her high school. As she completed five years of writing, she started to find a website for publishing her short stories. And then she found writerfluence which give her chance to participate and earn a page of their releasing book. She is so grateful to writerfluence for helping her in building career in writing.

Nowadays, she is working upon the release of her first novel that is "It wasn't my favour" a story of conflict between lover and bestfriend.

LoroseLorose

Nimi Kurian was born in Coonoor, Nilgiris. Her father was a tea planter and her mother a homemaker. She has two siblings. Her mother introduced her siblings and her to the world of books, while her father told them stories, some true and some, not so true. Her greatest memories of growing up in this picturesque town are going to the library and searching for fairies and goblins in the garden.

She went to school in St. Joseph's Convent, Coonoor, and graduated from Madras Christian College, Tambaram, Chennai. She has two post-graduate degrees from the University of Madras.

She retired after almost a quarter-century of working with Young World, the children's magazine brought out by The Hindu. She has published several books for children - Farmyard Tales, Christmas Held to Ransom, Magic in the Mountains, among others.

Back in the Nilgiri hills, she occupies her time writing.

Prakhar Patidar is a 22-year-old post-grad from Christ University trying to make it into the professional world of stories and wrap her head around the fact that groceries are expensive.

Her tantrums as a kid were more often than not met with stories her mom cooked up to deal with them. That's where she feels it all began. When she asked for a candy every night before bed, she got jaggery instead with a story of this mouse that bought it every night. One could only have a small piece, or else the mouse would run away. When she demanded to be told five stories every night before bed, her mom complied and made up stories, at least, till she hit writer's-block. Then a tantrum for five new stories meant widened eyes and "You listen to one story and go to bed, or you sleep outside the house."

This fascination with and love for stories has

shaped all her major academic and professional choices. She is currently exploring different genres and forms with her creative writing by using "call for submissions" on various platforms as a prompt. Rubatosis, her contribution to the book FemmeFluenza is a happy result of this creative exploration. Similar to the anthology she has recently compiled: Shahar. It brings together the myriad of ways people have experienced different cities: one poetic or prosaic piece at a time. She looks forward to a professional career in academia or creative writing, whichever way life takes her. You can find more of her work at I Did This With Words.

https://lookwhatididwithwords.wordpress.com/
About writing for FemmeFluenza, Prakhar say: "I had been wanting to tell this story [Rubatosis] for a while now and I can gladly say FemmeFluenza proved to be a great opportunity to be able to do so. I appreciate WriteFluenza's initiatives to amass new voices and give them a platform."

R aised and residing in Bengaluru, Rashmi Navada has a Master's in Computer Applications. After spending most of her young years traversing the Bengaluru traffic and attending late-night client calls, she quit the IT industry to pursue her interest in travel.

Being a voracious reader, writing comes naturally to her. Not wishing to get back to the corporate grind, she now works as a freelance writer, writing articles on health and relationships.

When not trying to manage her young twin girls, she writes short fiction.

Sakshvii is the brain-child of young talent, Varshini Nainar. She is well-versed in writing creative stories. She desires to take place in everyone's heart through her irreplaceable words. Her ideas towards imagination strengthen the structure of her writing. She is currently a freelance content writer. She had published a book called 'The Tale of the Kismet' with her co-author Sakthi Subramanian. The story is a romantic-thriller that grasp the quick attention of the young generation. She has also participated in various competitions in online forums, and her works were published on their websites. Her story has been a part of the 'Spectrum of thoughts' anthology. She is maintaining accounts in various forums under her pen-name 'Sakshvii' such as In-kitt, Penana etc. To spread her words along with her love to the readers, she is handling a page, @sakshvii_, on Instagram.

Sharda Mishra is an avid reader, a hiker, and a photographer, from Ranchi, India. Studying human emotions is her passion. She is a mother of two lovely daughters. Sharda Mishra loves to pen down her thoughts about social issues. She believes that humor should be the way of life. She finds talking to children very cathartic. She loves cooking and tweaking recipes. She eats with her eyes and loves food photography. She is in IT but her fondness is in writing. She has been happily married for twenty years and lives with her husband and two lovely daugfhters.

Her mother was a homemaker and father worked as a manager in a bank. Sharda has always been influenced by her mother's strong personality and kindness in every area of her life.

Sharda's love for reading came from rummaging for books and magazines, which was a scarce thing for her, growing up. She never had the privilege of owning a book of her own, up until she was an adult, and thus the hunger of reading kept growing. She holds a Bachelor's degree in Public Administration and Computer Applications and Masters in Computer Applications.

Understanding human emotions has always been her passion and she expresses that through her writing. Exploring human feelings has always intrigued her empathy towards every living being. Most of the ideas and thoughts in her stories come from talking to people. Talking to children and understanding human emotions through their eyes makes her realize the simplicity of life and how to achieve happiness even in diverse situations.

Sneha Acharekar is a passionate logophile, an avid reader, a complete movie buff and a singer in places that reverberate. In that order. She has been writing since her school days – stories and poems for her school magazine. An active blogger and poetess on various online sites, her articles have made it to the featured lists on platforms as Momspresso, Women's Web and YourQuote.

As of today, Acharekar has three published books

to her name. Based on the genre of dark romance, her first fiction novel Faith, Fate and a Fairytale (2017) is the closest to her heart. Her first book in the non-fiction genre – Let Go, Yet Glow – was published in January 2014 under a pseudonym KaTHaa. Purple Winters (2020) is the third of her books which is a collection of 150 free verses.

Acharekar came up with Stories by Sneha in 2020 – a podcast that plays on all podcasting channels viz. AnchorFM, Spotify, Apple Podcasts, Google Podcasts, Hubhopper, KukuFM, RadioPublic, Castbox, Breaker, to name a few. The podcast features short stories written and narrated by Acharekar and she successfully managed to cross over 30k listens overall – that being a good number considering the span and the popularity of the medium with Indian listeners.

In 2021, she has also had her poems published in the poetry collection 'Spent' and a short story published in 'Wafting Earthy'; by WriteFluence.

Acharekar is currently working on content for Season 2 of Stories by Sneha that will begin sometime soon in 2021. If you're a writer and want your story to reach a relatively large listener's base, reach out to her on her Instagram handle @the.agathist

Snehal Amembal had an affinity towards books from a very young age. Her earliest memory of her connection with books is of sitting in front of an old wooden cabinet, greedily poring over her books ; deciding which one to choose.

When growing up she enjoyed writing essays as part of her school work and it was in high school that she first started writing poetry. She has written ever since and even prefers texting to calling.

Snehal holds two Masters Degrees - Organisational Psychology from the University of Mumbai and Human Resources Management from the London School Of Economics & Political Science. She worked within HR departments in India and UK across the retail, leisure and private healthcare sectors for 8 years before she transitioned into becoming a mum.

She currently is a blogger and poet based in London with her husband and two toddlers. Her writing primarily reflects her motherhood journey. She also reviews books authored by writers of South Asian heritage on her blog Desi Lekh.

Snehal has an infectious laugh and a very loud mind. She believes that observation might just be her superpower.

∞ ∞ ∞

Udita Mukherjee lives in Kolkata, India. She completed her B.Sc. (Hons) in Economics from Presidency University in 2020. Her first play was selected for The Theatre Project 2020 by Bombay Theatre Company. It is titled 'Appendix' and can be found in the IGTV section of Bombay Theatre Company's Instagram. She loves writing poems and short stories. Currently, she is working on her second novel. Her favourite authors include Agatha Christie, Oscar Wilde, Virginia Woolf, Roald Dahl, Amitav Ghosh. She hopes her work can reflect the constant crazy characterizing her imagination. She draws inspiration from her daily interactions with the natural and the supernatural. Most of her plots present themselves to her in dreams and nightmares.

Uma Fenton grew up in Durgapur, a well-planned city in West Bengal. It is from this place that her interest in art and literature began and developed. She has always been able to express herself better through writing. She is a graduate in engineering and has a Master's degree in Theological studies. Uma has a formal training in martial arts and believes in fitness. She's also the founder of Hearts and Hands Foundation: A Social Welfare Trust working towards the welfare of the underprivileged. She currently resides in the city of Hyderabad, with her husband and two children and works as a freelance writer. Apart from writing, she enjoys reading and watching football.

Vaishali Chandorkar Chitale is an alumna of the Indian Institute of Mass Communication, New Delhi. She is an English (Hons) graduate from Hindu College, Delhi University. A free-lance journalist and writer, she likes to write about her life, anecdotes and fiction.She has lately taken to pen lyrical poems too.Her stories have been published on online platforms of www.StoryMirror.comandwww.Bonobology.com. Her story, 'Romancing the Husband' has been published in the Impish Lass anthology, 'Dating After Death'. She has taught English in many schools and retired from Delhi Public school, Pune in 2004 after a career of over 14 years to follow her passion for writing.

You can follow her on her blog-anenviablejouney.wordpress.com

She can be reached at vchandorkar@gmail.com

Vini kunhappan was born to a Malayali father and a Maharashtrian mother in the desert country of Dubai. U.A.E. Her basic education was completed in the gulf at Progressive English School. When her family decided to move back to Mumbai,India; where she completed her higher education in Icles college Navi mumbai. She currently works as a primary teacher in Radcliffe school kharghar Navi Mumbai, which is something she is extremely passionate about. Her tryst with writing started at an early age. She has a credible number of articles, poems,and stories published on various online platforms and websites. She had taken a sabbatical from her passion for writing for around 10yrs. She thanks the lockdown for giving her time to revive her passion for writing. She is a teacher by day and writer by night. She is also a blogger writing for WriteFluence and also her personal blog vinni's adda, where she writes her mind out.

www.ingramcontent.com/pod-product-compliance
Lightning Source LLC
Chambersburg PA
CBHW061514120726
48001CB00004B/1312